TIL DEATH DO US PART

RICHARD OSBORN

This is a work of fiction. The events and characters described herein are imaginary and are not intended to refer to specific places or living persons. The opinions expressed in this manuscript are solely the opinions of the author and do not represent the opinions or thoughts of the publisher. The author has represented and warranted full ownership and/or legal right to publish all the materials in this book.

Til Death Do Us Part
All Rights Reserved.
Copyright © 2015 Richard Osborn
v3.0 r2.0

Cover Photo © 2015 thinkstockphotos.com. All rights reserved - used with permission.

This book may not be reproduced, transmitted, or stored in whole or in part by any means, including graphic, electronic, or mechanical without the express written consent of the publisher except in the case of brief quotations embodied in critical articles and reviews.

Outskirts Press, Inc.
http://www.outskirtspress.com

ISBN: 978-1-4787-5657-6

Outskirts Press and the "OP" logo are trademarks belonging to Outskirts Press, Inc.

PRINTED IN THE UNITED STATES OF AMERICA

To

*Tish
Mark Katie Jennie Kyle
My Family
Whom I love very much*

Acknowledgement

This book is my first and I have to acknowledge the person who pushed me forward.

Professor Cass Dalglish,
Augsburg College, Minneapolis, Minnesota

B.A. The College of St. Catherine
M.F.A. Vermont College of Fine Arts
Ph.D. The Union Institute

I am grateful to Cass for the time she spent with me in my Creative Writing education. She had me cut and paste, delete, rewrite, cut and paste, develop further. One time I did not want to follow her instructions because I wanted a certain part of a story included in the work. She said to me, "You know, sometimes you are really stubborn."

On the day of my graduation in June 2009, Cass came to me, handed me a notebook and said, "Keep on writing." I have.

I am grateful to Augsburg College in Minneapolis, Minnesota for giving me the opportunity to complete my education, which was interrupted by the Vietnam War. Since graduation, I have tutored at The Christo Rey Jesuit High School in Minneapolis, tutored individual students, and helped high school seniors prepare their college essays.

Thank you, Cass for the kick in the pants which moved me forward. I'm having a great time.

Rich Osborn

There are things you do because you want to.

There are things you do because you have to.

— Holiday Mathis

Prologue

He walked down the Via dei Mercanti in Milan, passing his locked Fiat Sport 500 parked in front. He entered the building, went up the stairs. Entering his flat, he walked down the hall toward the bedroom. Inside the room on the left was his closet. He opened the door. On the back wall were moldings behind each shelf. The center shelf had only lightweight clothing stored on it. He reached in, removed the clothing, lifted up on the shelf, and removed it to expose the shelf supports. The right bracket acted as a lever; when raised, it released a latch to a sliding door. He raised the lever. After he had slid the door open, he reached in the compartment. The two items he wanted were his 9mm pistol and a box of shells. He slid the panel closed and heard it lock. He replaced the shelf and the clothes. He took the shells and his pistol, packed them in a briefcase, and went down to his car. He locked the case in the trunk, got in, and drove off.

One

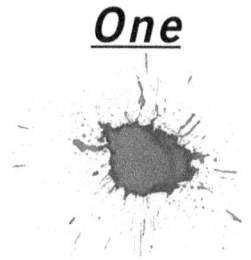

It's a quiet happy hour for a Wednesday. Usually Jake's is buzzing with the voices of the after-work crowd with music heard softly in the background. Aaron Kelley loved this place — his respite between work and home, he often said. The wood paneling and soft lighting gave it an atmosphere of elegance, and best of all, no smoking. He came here mostly three times a week but always at least twice. Max, the bartender, knew him well and would grab the Chivas, rocks, twist, sometimes handing it to him before he even sat down. An outgoing man in his late 50's, he resembles Wally the Bartender in *Men's Health* magazine; easy to talk to, gives advice to anyone who asks, but you had to ask.

Aaron, a bachelor of 42 years, lives a fixed but comfortable lifestyle. His twin sister, Sharon, is married. She, her husband, and three children live about 30 minutes away and he sees them often. He is well off financially, buying property on the Virgin Islands of St. Thomas and St. John, vacationing there a couple of times a year, renting them when he wasn't. He never married, although he did want to in his earlier years. He liked women, but his education and career seemed to be important and got in the way. Somehow, it never worked out for him. The right one never appeared. He dated many but few excited him as a permanent mate. He would love to be a father and raise a child, especially a girl. He lives on the top floor of an open, roomy apartment with two bedrooms and a den located in an upscale neighborhood. The open concept kitchen gives him a feeling of being in an apartment, but not isolated in a room, allowing him to enjoy the superb view of the city. Many of his friends enjoy it when he entertains at his home and always comment on the contentment with which he surrounds himself.

A dermatologist by profession, he graduated from Princeton at the top of his class. He went on to study dermatology at Washington University in St. Louis, Missouri, completing his residency at Yale University's Department of Dermatology, the number-one dermatology residency program in the United States. He would sometimes come to Jake's with a colleague. If he was alone, he brought his best friend, his iPhone. If not at Jake's, he would be at the gym doing his aerobic workout and weight training to keep toned. He had an above-average physique, a clean-cut guy, always taking good care of himself, keeping his weight down with no special diet, just moderation. He could appear on the front cover of any men's magazine with his razor-sharp looks. His drinking habits were well controlled but he loved his scotch. When not going to Jake's he would go home from the gym, have one and only one in the evening before dinner, and watch the news — a ritual he never left out.

This night was different. He saw a woman sitting at a table in the opposite corner. She had been there several times the last couple of weeks. She was beautiful with her strawberry-blonde hair done up in a bun in the back and smooth skin — something a dermatologist observes. Although he would like to meet her, he knew he probably wouldn't. The idea of going up to a woman and making some small talk was not his style. Besides, she sat next to an Italian-looking man with a fat unlit cigar in his mouth. He appeared trim, fit with a strong five-o'clock shadow, and impeccably dressed. Somehow, the cigar didn't fit a man of his style. He would expect it to be "worn" by an older fat man with a big belly about twenty years her senior. They talked to each other, so Aaron thought for sure he was either her husband or maybe just someone she knew. Aaron casually raised his cell phone and took a picture of them. As he left, he looked at her and smiled. She returned the favor. He could smell the scent of her perfume. It was fragrant, feminine, and mild; not overwhelming like insect spray. Progress, he thought. Maybe next time I'm here, something will work out. It was an early evening for him as he had appointments and surgery the next morning.

Two

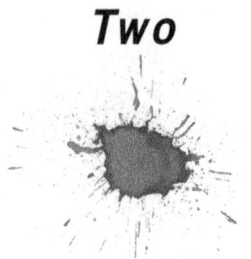

Morning came, his alarm awakening him with the usual soft guitar music. With coffee on auto-start the night before, he did his shave, shower, and sunscreen aftershave. He added a bagel or English muffin, and after, walked to the bus stop a block away. Many of his coworkers kidded him about being a physician with a late-model BMW in the garage, and yet taking the bus. He liked it and always said, "I just wanna be one of the ordinary." Besides, he hated traffic. Since leaving Jake's the night before, his mind had become obsessed with the woman at the corner table and her scent he'd picked up as he passed her on his departure. He thought of her as "the lady in the corner." He relished the face and smile. Her appeal fascinated him. Several weeks went by, returning to Jake's on a routine basis. He sat where he could see the table she regularly occupied, but for the entire month of June, she did not show up. A feeling of sadness came over him, as he was confident he would never see her again as her disappearance became prolonged. Story of my life, he thought.

On a Friday evening in late July, Aaron attended a fundraiser at the Athletic Club sponsored by the Society of Dermatology Awareness (SODA) — a strange acronym for a medical society. Suddenly, his face had an "Oh My God" expression. As he spoke with some of his colleagues, he looked up, and there she was across the room: "the lady in the corner." When he saw her he smiled, took a deep breath, and sighed to himself. Aaron lost interest in the conversation with some of his colleagues from out of town and a couple classmates from medical school. He kept an eye on her. He thought, even though I don't know this woman, I like her, and I am so pleased to see her again. She didn't see him immediately, but after a few minutes their eyes met, her head moved slightly, and a smile followed. Ah! he thought; a perfect time to make an introduction. She looked tanned and fit. The past few months obviously had been good to her. She was across the room with the same man she had been with at Jake's. He was tall, good-looking with a perpetual five-o'clock shadow, and very Italian. Was he her husband? They made a striking couple. Again, he had a fat unlit cigar in his mouth. Aaron never saw it lit, so he wondered if he used the same one all the time. He probably slept with it. But more important, why were they there? Was he a physician? Was he a dermatologist? Were they contributors to SODA? What was the connection? So many questions entered his mind, but he became determined to meet her.

Aaron excused himself, went to the bar, and ordered another Chivas. As he stood there, the woman went outside on the patio overlooking the lake. He turned and looked so he followed her, watching her straight back, narrow waist, nicely rounded hips, and long shapely legs. Walking was the first time he saw her other than sitting; she was tall. The thought came to his mind, *kick off those heels, honey; we'll fit.* His smile became locked and solid with a sigh of excitement from his lungs as he made his way to the patio. He approached, turning his head slightly toward her, and she did the same. The almost calm wind placed the fragrance of her to him. Wonderful, he thought, I love the scent.

"It's a *beautiful* evening," he said, starting a conversation.

"Yes, I became warm, so I decided to get some fresh air. I love the night with no moon, just brilliant stars," she said as he noticed a slight accent.

"My name is Aaron Kelley."

"I'm Maria Beldenado, a pleasure to meet you," as she extended her right hand. It was firm, skin smooth, and her nails perfectly manicured.

"Thank you, the pleasure is mine," he responded.

She wore a simple yellow dress, very little makeup, if any, and a diamond pendant on a silver chain around her neck. On the ring finger of her left hand she wore a gold band, no diamond. It appeared the thickness of string.

"I used to see you at Jake's at Belmont Square, but I haven't seen you there for at least a month or so." Aaron gave a slight tip of his head, a slight raising of his eyebrows, and a smile.

She looked delighted and said, "We've been out of town, in fact, in Italy for a relaxing holiday."

"Oh! How fantastic. I love Italy. I've vacationed, or as you say, I've gone on holiday to Monterosso. It is very beautiful and the food superb, not to mention the wines."

"Yes, we rent a residence every year at the Villa Lugari Cinque Terra on the Amalfi Coast near Portofino spending the third week in June through the second week of July just relaxing, enjoying the Mediterranean, with some wonderful Italian wine and cuisine. We always rent the same villa overlooking the Mediterranean. We've done it for several years, and it's just north of Monterosso."

"That's why you have such a beautiful tan, but be careful. Do you wear sunscreen?"

"I'll bet you're a dermatologist," she said. They looked at each other with a grin. Aaron turned around, resting his hips on the railing, folding his arms in front of his chest as he tilted his head back. They both laughed.

"Yes I am. What gave you the first clue, the fact that I'm at a SODA fundraiser?"

The night air was velvet and the stars brilliant. The sound of the crowd inside the club made Aaron game for wishing he were alone with her somewhere else. He was extremely attracted to her.

"May I ask: Is the gentleman you're with your husband, the man with a cigar?"

"Yes, he is," revealing a smile and hesitation as if she wanted to say more.

"The first time I saw you with him was at Jake's. Is he also a dermatologist?"

"No, he works in the medical field in Milan so we often go to events and conventions."

Aaron started to feel uncomfortable by asking so much information all at once. I'd better slow down and allow her to carry the ball a little, he thought.

A silence followed; neither seemed to know what to say.

"He's with me constantly. He's leaving for Milan tomorrow night for two weeks of conferences and presentations."

"Will you be going with him?"

"No, I plan to stay at the hotel and just do whatever I want. I'm going to shop, go to the workout room, relax, sit at the sidewalk cafés, sip wine, and read." She gazed up at the stars. It was a calm moment as her two weeks of solitude took over her mind.

The same thoughts riddled through Aaron's mind. He'd liked her at first sight. He felt a rush come through his body realizing he wanted to have some time with her.

"I will be joining him in Milan in two weeks."

"I know we just met and please don't think I am pushy or rude, but I'd like to invite you to dinner while he's gone." He paused. "If you would rather not, please say so."

"Oh, there you are!" The group she had been talking with interrupted the moment by coming out on the patio.

"We wondered where you were," one of them said. "Come join us. We want you to meet someone your husband is conversing with."

Aaron smiled as she turned, but it was a forced smile of disappointment as the question was not answered.

She turned, started to leave, looked back and said, "I'd like that."

Three

Aaron woke the next morning, did his usual routine, and left for the 7 a.m. bus stop. There was coolness in the late July air, which felt good as the days were warm and humid. Daylight stayed up late with the setting sun after 9 p.m. Summer is so pleasant, but the fall had its refreshing days also. He felt an inner calmness, a self-assurance and serenity as he walked briskly, a feeling he had not experienced for some time. He decided to give Maria a couple of days to relax away from her husband before he contacted her. He wanted to take it very slow but methodical. The bus arrived on time with the usual "Good morning, Aaron" greeting from the driver, who knew him well. Aaron asked him some time ago not to address him as "Doctor."

Maria woke early as the sun was just peeking above the horizon into their bedroom. They occupied a penthouse suite at the Belmont Hotel with a 270-degree view of the city. She loved the feeling of having met Aaron the evening before. *Refreshing* and *charming* are the words she thought about to describe him; very handsome. She decided to let her husband sleep, so she dressed in sweats and a loose-fitting shirt, left him a note, grabbed a water bottle, and headed to the workout room. No one else was there that hour of the morning so she started on the treadmill. The window faced east. She had a great view of the sunrise in a clear sky. An airplane in the distance streaked across the sky, climbing from the airport to somewhere. She thought of Roberto leaving later in the day. Life is good, she thought. I will have a whole two weeks to myself and look forward to some time with Aaron. He seems like a very nice man and very handsome. He's just a friend, she thought. No harm intended.

Aaron worked at the clinic in the morning and went to a sidewalk café nearby for lunch with one of his colleagues, always sitting in the shade where possible. He never was a sun worshiper. He ordered an Arnie Palmer. The day turned out warm with a slight breeze while he ate the lunch special of grilled scallops on a bed of greens, which were indeed simple, not filling, but hearty.

"You seem very alert and happy today," his colleague remarked. "My wife and I couldn't go last night to the SODA event. We had to attend a school concert the kids were in. Anybody interesting there?"

"Oh yes, yes indeed. I met several new people I had never known."

"Any singles?"

"Not that I know of, I think I was the only one."

"Think it will ever change?"

"Don't know. I haven't given up. Being single has some advantages, but it doesn't bother me."

They finished their meal, no dessert, just coffee, and started walking back to the clinic. It was a beautiful day and good to get out.

Maria accompanied Roberto to the hotel lobby. It was 3 p.m. and his flight left at 7. They embraced a good-bye as the UBER driver loaded his baggage in the trunk of the limousine.

"I will call you every day between nine and ten each morning. It will be between four and five in the afternoon in Milan."

"Yes, thank you. I will look forward to hearing from you. I will plan on it," she replied.

They smiled and waved as the car departed. Maria strolled back into the hotel.

A couple of days later, Aaron called her at the Belmont. There was no answer at her room so he left a voice mail telling her he would be at Jake's around 6 p.m. if she would care to join him. He gave her his iPhone number and asked her to leave a text. Around 4 p.m., she replied she would be there. He was delighted and eager to have the next two hours go by faster.

Four

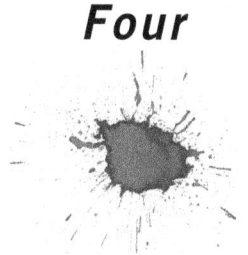

The walk to Jake's took about 15 minutes, so he left the office 20 minutes early. It was such a nice afternoon. He wished Maria was with him, but she would be soon and he could introduce plans for the time her husband was away. His Chivas was in his hand before he sat down. Max never failed him.

Aaron had some thoughts cross his mind. I have never felt this way in my life. I have a feeling for someone for the first time. Of course, she had to be married. Life has not ever been simple.

Maria arrived promptly at 6. Aaron stood, greeted her with a handshake she proposed. He knew a man does not offer his hand. It is a lady who reaches out. Always cognizant of proper etiquette, he prided himself on practicing it. The perfume she wore was again fascinating, almost hypnotizing. She ordered a glass of Hendry, an unoaked chardonnay from Napa Valley. It surprised him she didn't order an Italian wine.

"Well, how was your day?" he asked.

"Marvelous! I woke up when I wanted, went to the workout room, ate a light breakfast, dressed, and went on a shopping stroll. I said good-bye to Roberto two days ago. It has felt so good to be alone."

"Does your husband — I'm sorry I don't know his name — keep tabs on you and deny you this type of freedom?"

"His name is Roberto. He's Italian, born and raised in Milan, and he still has family living there. He does have a hold on me. We married fifteen years ago in 1999, so I have become accustomed to it even though I resent it." She hesitated. "Or better yet, I hate it."

"Have you thought about leaving him?"

"Yes I have, but I can't. He needs me."

For what? Aaron wondered.

A feeling of heartache came over him, not knowing what it would be like to be in a relationship in which you would not be happy.

They sat, made some small-talk conversation, and ordered another round of scotch and wine.

"Listen, tomorrow is Friday. Would you be interested in having a casual dinner?"

"Oh yes, I'd like to. I don't know the city very well, so let's do it."

Aaron felt elated, and she gave him a nice smile while moving her head "yes."

"Also, on Saturday afternoon, I have symphony tickets. We could have a more formal dinner after."

"Sounds wonderful. I'll cancel everything on my empty calendar." They both laughed and smiled together.

"Good! I'll plan to pick you up at the hotel tomorrow at 6, if it's a good time for you?"

"Perfect."

"Dress is casual. I'll send you a text as I'm leaving my apartment as I am about 5 minutes away. Then on Saturday, I'll pick you up at 1. The concert begins at 2 and, by the way" — Aaron hesitated, smiling — "may I ask what the perfume is you are wearing?"

Maria rolled her head back, gave him a chuckle and a smile, and said, "Not at all. It's Chanel No. 5, my favorite. Sometimes I splurge and get a quarter-ounce bottle; it's so expensive."

"It's very beautiful and feminine. It suits you perfectly."

By then they had had a second round of drinks, and the conversation continued as casual. Aaron felt so relaxed with her, and it showed she was enjoying the same. They left Jake's about 8 p.m. and stopped at a local pizzeria for a quick snack. He walked her back to the Belmont. The night was dark now. The days were getting shorter. She thanked him for a lovely time and looked forward to the symphony and dinner on Saturday. He walked back to his apartment, had one smaller Chivas, and went to bed. Life is looking good, he thought.

Five

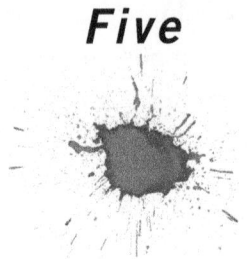

Friday was routinely a half day of work for Aaron. The clinic closed at 1 p.m., and he enjoyed Friday afternoon as he could go to the athletic club, play some handball, or do a spinning class or swim, but always finished with yoga. There was usually someone wanting to play handball looking for a partner. He usually didn't go to Jake's on Fridays because of too many people and thundering conversation.

Aaron looked forward to his evening with Maria. He arrived in his BMW promptly at six after texting her to let her know he was on his way. She looked stunning, even for casual attire. The door attendant escorted her to the car, opening the door. Her Chanel No. 5 was intoxicating. Aaron loved it. These next two weeks are going to be fun, he thought to himself as Maria sat down and fastened her seatbelt. Unfortunately, two days have already gone.

The evening went very well as they shared a few laughs, a casual meal, and a bottle of fine Italian wine. They spoke of their travels and Aaron's properties in St. Thomas and St. John in the Virgin Islands. She had never been there but it interested her as to what made it attractive.

"I'm going down to St. John next month for at least a week, maybe two. You should come with me."

Smiling, she replied, "I would love to, but..." Her sentence ended abruptly and Aaron understood.

On the way back to the hotel, Aaron played in his mind whether or not to invite her to his apartment but decided it would be a bit too premature. At the hotel, the same door attendant came to the car and opened the door. Maria thanked Aaron for a pleasant evening, put her hand on his right arm, leaned over, and gave him a kiss on the cheek. Holy shit! Aaron thought. Nice gesture!

He didn't go directly home. Instead, he decided to drive, stop, and sit by the river to contemplate. Why the kiss on the cheek? What did it mean? So many questions and so much excitement he never experienced in life. It might have been a European way of saying, "I enjoyed it; thank you." Go slow, Aaron, go slow; I think I could fall in love with Maria.

On Saturday, Aaron again sent Maria a text to let her know he was on his way. He arrived at 1 p.m., just as she was coming out of the hotel with the assistance of the doorman. Aaron complimented her again on how wonderful she looked wearing her yellow dress she had worn at the SODA event. He enjoyed her Chanel. They sped away to the Center for Entertainment Arts to hear a concert followed by dinner. The concert over, they strolled along the river in the late-afternoon sun. She reached over and took Aaron's hand. He smiled, and his whole body seemed to melt in the sunrise of their relationship. Dinner reservations were at 7 p.m. at Louie's 510, the most upscale restaurant in the city. He felt very happy. He thought, Yes, I think I could fall in love.

Six

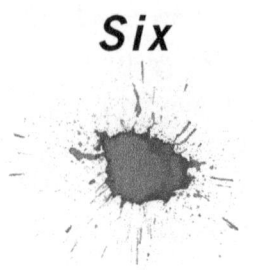

At dinner, the conversation took a different tone. Aaron wanted to know more about the relationship between Maria and Roberto. He let her lead the way.

She started talking plainly and more openly. She married Roberto fifteen years ago. Aaron could tell the spark in her was somewhat gone, or was it? Would Maria like to get out from under the hook of marriage? It became an engaged communication. There seemed to be a sense of a comfort level between them. Aaron found himself speaking more freely about his practice in dermatology and his financial investments. He loved having his properties in St. Thomas and St. John. The rental agency he works through keeps the vacationers coming. He experiences few vacancies but always reserves a week about three times a year to go to St. John just to get away. It's much quieter than St. Thomas.

"He was a different man when I first met him," she said. "He was kind, a nonsmoker, and very rich. He showered me with gifts which I could never afford. No one had ever treated me like this. It was a new beginning. It's just like meeting you. You are such a gentleman: polite, articulate, and obviously taking good care of yourself physically and financially."

"Do you have any children?" Aaron asked.

"No, we don't. He never wanted any. I would have loved to have had a boy and a girl, but it got to the point where I couldn't even bring up the subject. I sometimes wish he wasn't my husband."

Aaron felt a rush through his body. He had never felt this way toward a female before, and at that very moment, he knew he wanted her as his wife.

"May I ask how old you are? You look very young," he said.

"I am 42 and am afraid I'm past my childbearing years. And you?"

"I'm also 42, and not past my childbearing years, if you know what I mean."

Maria sat there with a big grin. She knew exactly what he meant.

Aaron thought, we would have been so much better a couple than what she now has, if what she says is for real. I wish she were single, and we just met.

The meal was delicious; the wine, a $250 bottle of a 2007 Solaia, a premier Italian, could only be described as superb. Aaron was instrumental in establishing an upscale wine cellar at Louie's 510. He made some large donations, encouraged other patrons to do the same, so he received a 50% discount on wines. The $250 bottle cost $125.

The conversation tended to stay within the category of their lives. She received her undergraduate degree from the European University Geneva and continued studies at the University of Strasbourg in Strasbourg, Alsace, France. She spoke three languages fluently: Italian, her primary, English, and French.

Aaron realized he had 10 more days to be with her, and he became determined he would make the best of it. Maria would be leaving for Milan on the fourteenth day. He wondered if he was experiencing what it was like to fall in love with someone. He decided to make plans for their final weekend. He met with her after work, but not at Jake's. He did not want any of the regulars, especially Max the bartender, to recognize her with him or him with her — whichever applied. Maria met Aaron for lunch a couple of days, and they had dinner each night, followed by a stroll along the river. They attended a baseball game, which she did not understand, but the worst was football, not known in her country because it's fútbal in Italy and soccer in the United States. Time was rapidly closing. Aaron realized push would come to shove. He had to let his feelings be known to her, so he thought for their final time together, it would be nice to be out of town.

The weekend came. Maria would be taking the 7 p.m. Alitalia flight to Milan on Monday. He proposed a plan and they decided to drive to the countryside for Saturday and Sunday, stopping at different towns and restaurants along the way. Aaron knew which places had the better cuisine. Two Tree Point B&B, known for its location, comfort, and good food was the stop on Saturday evening. Aaron reserved a junior suite for both of them a week ago. Maria did not object. The drive there was nice under a sunny sky, with little traffic, and some color starting to show on the trees. They arrived around 4 p.m., unpacked, and went to the cocktail lounge for a before-dinner libation. After dinner, they strolled across the grounds. Maria took Aaron's hand. They arrived at their cabin and sat on the deck sipping a Warre's 1966 vintage port. Conversation quieted, so Aaron decided to break the ice. Staring straight ahead he said, "So tell me what you like about staying with Roberto." A long pause presented itself with neither looking at the other.

"I did like and loved Roberto when I first met him. He was very kind to me, very rich, and I was, shall we say, vulnerable. I was 27, never married, and looked forward to a family. I spent most of my earlier life in college educating myself. Time passed me by, and now I realize it."

Aaron poured more port into her glass. The air was comfortable and the sunset beautiful with the sun just below the horizon. He knew enough wine or port usually becomes "truth serum."

"Do you still like him, or better yet, do you love him?"

After a long pause, "I don't know. I feel he needs me."

"'Needs you' is different than 'love.' So, he needs you for what? Do you need him? I'm the one who needs you. I've been alone for 42 years, and you're the first person to come into my life and give me any excitement and meaning. I believe there's a compatibility issue you and I seem to understand, and it's only taken me ten days to figure it out."

"I do have to say you have made a difference in my life toward a relationship with a person of the opposite sex. You are fun, gentlemanly, articulate, and most of all, you are kind to me."

"It's the Chanel No. 5, no question about it," looking at Maria with a smile.

They both laughed.

The sun had set, the sky a brilliant red, magenta and gold; the evening cool but not cold.

Aaron thought he would end the conversation; he turned to Maria and said, "If you were single, I would ask you to marry me in a heartbeat. Maria, I have come to an unconditional conclusion. I know I love you." Maria did not move. She sat there and took another sip of port. She did not know what to say. It seemed an eternity. She looked at Aaron, hesitated for about five seconds, and said, "I love you too."

Aaron stood slowly, took Maria by the hand, and invited her up beside him. They embraced, and the kiss was long and meaningful. He started to slip his hand toward her breast, but she gently placed it down next to his waist.

"I-I-I can't do that. It would be unfair to Roberto. Besides, I took a vow of *for better, for worse, until death do us part.* Roberto thinks the vow was: *for better, for worse, until lunch do us part.* I can't break my side of the vow."

Smiles broke out with both of them. Aaron, however, stepped back, and with a serious look on his face addressed the issue. "Nonsense! Divorce him, and let's get on with our lives, just the two of us. You and I are meant for each other, but just happened to meet at the wrong time in life."

"I stay because, like I said, he needs me, and I took a vow!" Maria's hands surrounded her head.

Silence ensued, and they had a fixed gaze on each other.

The conversation ended. They finished their port and retired to bed. Maria changed into her nightgown in the bathroom. Meanwhile, Aaron slipped on a pair of running shorts. He always slept bare-chested.

"Don't you wear pajamas?"

"No. Pajamas are what newlyweds keep on the side of the bed in case of fire," Aaron replied, smiling.

Maria looked puzzled.

He realized Maria didn't understand. Aaron turned out the bed stand light and they said "good night" to each other. Turning toward her, he could see her silhouette with the full moon shining brightly through the window. A few moments later Maria turned her head toward him. She leaned over and kissed him. Aaron gently put his arm under her and she slid her body over to him resting her head on his right shoulder. Aaron, his arm under her back, kissed her on the hair of her head. Her scent smelled wonderful and they fell asleep together.

Seven

Aaron woke with the sun shining in the room. He sat up on the side of the bed; it was just after 8:30. The smell of Maria and Channel No.5 filled his nostrils and head with gratification. What a wonderful way to go to bed, he thought. He looked at her sleeping; I love her. He put the coffee pot on and walked across the room toward the bathroom picking up some clean clothes on the way. He decided to shower, shave and get ready for breakfast before heading home. As he dried himself out of the shower, he heard Maria talking on the phone. The conversation was in Italian. He realized it was Roberto in Milan. The communication sounded civil, and it appeared Roberto did all the talking. Aaron waited. The conversation over, he left the bathroom and saw her sitting up in bed gazing out the window at the morning fog in the valley. Aaron said nothing.

"He's called me every day at about this time. It's 4:00 in the afternoon in Milan. He said he was so looking forward to my returning to him."

Aaron didn't react, but said, "I'm going out to get the morning paper. I'll be right back."

He went to the entry door, unlocked it, picked up the morning paper, closed the door and said, "I'm back." They both smiled and laughed. It was a fun moment. "I'm going out on the deck to have a cup of coffee and read the paper. Why don't you get ready and we'll head over to breakfast?"

Maria showered, changed into comfortable clothes and went out on the deck. She came up behind Aaron, put her hands on his cheeks and chin, tilted his head back and kissed him upside down on the lips. "Thank you for a wonderful time and a wonderful vacation shall we say, and an equally enjoyable evening." She bent over and gave him a kiss on the forehead. With tears in her eyes, she smiled, and said, "Thank you." Aaron only smiled back enjoying the excitement they had experienced that weekend.

Breakfast finished, they checked out and started the trip back to the city. It was quiet with only smiles between them and occasional geographical conversation. As they approached the outskirts of the city, Maria spoke.

"I have not seen your apartment. Is it presentable?"

"It is, and I would love to take you there. I have a beautiful view of the river, the city, and the airport in the distance. I also have a wonderful 1997 Italian red from the Piedmont region. Shall we head there?"

"Oh Yum! Yes, let's go" was her reply.

Aaron felt a closer excitement in being with her. How she'd introduced the idea was enlightening and refreshing. He had avoided an invitation so as not to be forward or suggestive. It was mid-afternoon, a beautiful July day. The arrival at the apartment gave Aaron the feeling of walking in with his wife. He loved it.

"Oh my! This is beautiful," she said, her eyes widening, head turning side to side.

"Thank you. I'm very happy here. Please come out on my balcony."

They walked through the living room and toward the French doors leading outside. The table, chairs, and umbrella had the look of a page from *Architectural Digest*. The view gave a feeling of relaxation and elegance. It was breathtaking.

"Do you dine out here?" she asked.

"Almost every day. Should we order something for dinner and enjoy your last evening with dinner on the deck?"

"Wonderful! And I will have that glass of wine, as long as you said 'it's Italian' and I love the United States flag gently flying in the breeze."

They both smiled at each other and chuckled. Aaron did have Italian. It was a special moment. He looked at her squarely in the face, putting his hands on her shoulders. He spoke slowly.

"I — love — you — Maria."

"I know, Aaron, I know." A long pause. "And I — love — you — Aaron."

They embraced, kissed, and held each other for a minute or so.

Aaron ordered from the local deli, had it delivered. They ate and sat, finishing the bottle of Italian red. He decided to not again get sexually involved with her. He wanted her to leave feeling good about what they'd accomplished; no guilt. He planted the grain of thought. It would grow if she let it.

Dinner over, they walked to the Belmont. He kissed her at the door and told her where the restaurant was for lunch tomorrow. Aaron canceled his appointments after 12 noon. He would be at the hotel at 3:00 to bid her farewell.

Eight

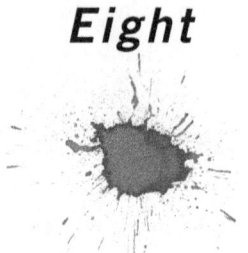

Aaron made his way to the bus the next morning. Even though he realized the success he was, he felt heavyhearted and knew life did not always give him a trump card. Entering the clinic, he told the receptionist to reschedule his afternoon. He had to leave the office by 12 p.m. and would not return until the next morning.

Bridget said, "Your schedule is heavy this afternoon."

"I know, and so is mine."

Bridget had never before seen Aaron in an agitated mood. Something must be on his mind, she thought. He seems upset.

He met Maria at the outdoor café on Stonehead Street just around the corner from the hotel. The lunch was casual and slow, Aaron telling the server they were in no hurry.

"May I take you to the airport? My afternoon is free."

Maria's head perked up, eyes widened, and a smile came to her face. "Oh, how lovely. It would be very nice."

They walked to Aaron's apartment, where he picked up the BMW, and drove together to the Belmont. The valet took the car to the parking garage and they went to her suite. Aaron took her already packed suitcases and went to the car while Maria checked out. The drive to the airport would take about 45 minutes, and they had plenty of time, so Aaron did not hurry.

Maria's phone rang promptly at 3:20 p.m. It had to be Roberto. It was.

"Buon pomeriggio Roberto. Io sono nella mia rubrica di limousine per l'aeroporto. Il mio volo è in orario, quindi mi aspetto di arrivare a

Milano domani mattina alle Sette quarantacinque." (Good afternoon, Roberto. I'm in my limo heading to the airport. My flight is on time, so I expect to arrive in Milan tomorrow morning at 7:45.)

They talked for about five minutes. Roberto said he would be there to meet her.

Arriving at the airport, Aaron parked, took the two cases, and walked with her to the ticket counter. It was a slow walk, and he expressed how much he would miss her. Maria took his arm and hugged her head to his shoulder. She checked her bags at the counter, and her boarding pass indicated seat 3A. Because she was in first class, security was a separate line and would be much faster, so they sat in a private corner of the airport, talked, and savored each moment as their last. They traded e-mail addresses. He was not to text her as Roberto would hear her phone make the sound of a text message coming in and would ask about it, or even worse, pick it up and read it. She had a separate e-mail address from Roberto's because of his business and clientele, so e-mail would be their only method of communication.

It was now time to say good-bye. They stood, embraced, and Maria started to sob. She placed her head on Aaron's shoulder; the tears made his shirt wet.

"I love you so much. I wish I could stay. It was a wonderful and exciting twelve days. Thank you, thank you." Aaron was speechless but was able to get out his thoughts. "I wish you could stay as well. This is the first time in my life I have loved someone with whom I would like to spend the rest of my life. I would encourage you to divorce him and we could be together, as you said, 'until death do us part.'"

They headed to the security line for first-class passengers. Maria went through, turned, waved, and threw Aaron a kiss. He returned to his car in the garage and felt very lonely. How could I change this? How could I make it work? He decided to go to St. John early and contact the leasing agent tomorrow to set up a week for him.

The evening went slow. He stopped at Jake's. Max asked where he had been as he hadn't seen him for the past two weeks.

"I've been in busy business." Yes, monkey business, he chuckled and thought to himself.

Aaron walked slowly back home, enjoying the evening air. He thought of Maria savoring a glass of wine as her Alitalia flight progressed toward Milan. He went to bed at the usual time but had difficulty getting to sleep. His thoughts were about Maria on the airplane. At some point, he dozed off and didn't realize it. He woke at 5 a.m. He knew it was 12 noon in Milan. He went to his computer and in his mailbox was her address in the inbox. He opened it.

Amò con Monica - Good Morning!

I'm here. The flight was fine, and seat 3B was open next to me. I wished many times you were here with me. Roberto met me at the airport with his car, driver, and cigar -J. I slept a good bit of the trip over. We're going to lunch. After a couple of glasses of wine, I will probably take a nap this afternoon and by tomorrow I should be back to normal. Roberto arranged for us to spend the next week at the Villa Lugari Cinque Terra, Portofino, our favorite retreat. I'm sure we will relax, but I will be thinking of you. Thank you again for the stirring and thrilling two weeks. I'll write again soon. Love you; miss you already!

Nine

Aaron called Alphonso, his leasing agent in St. John, and he answered promptly.

"Alfie!"

"Hey, Dr. Kelley, it's good to hear your voice. How are things going up north?"

"Fine Alfie, fine! Good to hear you as well. Fall is beginning to show, which means winter is just around the corner. I need to get away for a bit. How are the bookings either the end of this month or the first of next?"

"Interesting you should call today. The owner's suite reservations for the third and fourth week of this month have canceled, so it's wide open. Are you coming down?"

"Yes, reserve the fourth week for me. I need some R & R and just getaway time."

"You got it. It'll be good to see you."

"Thanks, Alfie. I'll be sure to stop by when I am there, and oh! I will call about a pickup at the St. Thomas airport. Bye for now."

"I'll wait for your call, no problem. Bye."

Aaron returned to his work at the clinic with much to take care of besides his work. He told his receptionist and nurse to reschedule all of his patients for the fourth week. He would be out of town. He called the airline, made his reservation, and then called Vincent, his condo manager, to let him know he would be arriving the fourth week of the month.

The month went by slowly, but Aaron pressed on knowing there would be an R & R light at the end of the tunnel very soon. He connected via e-mail with Maria regularly. She would send him a message in the morning so it would show up on his computer when he got up for the day. He would do the same just before he went to bed so she would have it when she got up. He learned from her about the villa in Portofino. It was the same one, always. She said Roberto was a victim of habit. He would, without exception, get up around 6 a.m., fix the coffee, walk to the newsstand three blocks away, unlit cigar in mouth, pick up the morning paper and return, sometimes stopping, buying a new cigar. Returning, he would sit on the patio in the early morning sunshine overlooking the Mediterranean, drinking his coffee, reading the *CORRIERE DELLA SERA*, the paper published in Milan, as well as *LA SCHERMO LUCCA*, published in Tuscany, followed by breakfast.

The week ended and Aaron went to the gym, did his workout, and headed home. He spent the weekend picking up the apartment, washing clothes, packing, and was ready for the UBER car to take him to the airport on Monday morning at 7 a.m. for his 9 a.m. departure. He was so excited to have met Maria. His mind was full of her and her Chanel No. 5.

Before Aaron went to bed, he sat down at his computer.

G'Mornin, darlin'. I wish you were here. I am leaving in the morning for one week at my villa on the island of St. John in the Caribbean. It's a quiet place overlooking the sea with my own private sandy beach. You would look nice sitting beside me in a bikini, mojito in hand doing nothing but quiet relaxation. There are some nice restaurants nearby and at Caneel Bay, a resort just a few miles away, they established a special place called Turtle Bay Estate House featuring fine cuisine and local fare. Please continue our e-mails. It is my morning joy to see you in my inbox. I LOVE you, and I MISS you. We MUST meet again, and soon.

Aaron

Ten

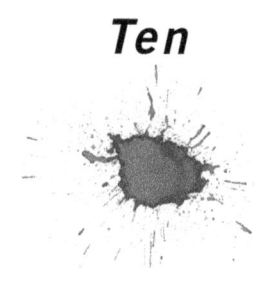

The guitar sound awakened Aaron from a deep sleep at 5:45 a.m. The coffee made, he poured himself a cup and readied up for his usual routine. Computer first, though, as he knew an e-mail would be there.

> *Hey, darlin' to you! It's been beautiful here, and I also wish you were here, or I there would be better. Roberto has been a real pain in the posterior these last few weeks as a client departed, and another is considering leaving. He can't stand to lose a client. Oh, how I wish I could get on the airplane with you, fly off to a new land, sit on the beach, and sip a mojito? I don't know what it is. No, maybe an Italian red would suit me better. I've never had a mojito and don't even know what's in it, but as long as you recommend it, I'd probably like it. I have no idea what your place is like so I expect to receive some photos. Yes, we do have to meet someday, and I want it to be soon. I wish Roberto weren't here, and we could get our lives together forever. Being with you was so freeing!*
>
> *Love you, Love you, Love you.*
> *Maria*

He didn't send a reply but would wait until he arrived in St. John. He went to shave, shower, and get dressed. Dress is always casual when he flies. No one knows him, and he could care less anyway. It would be a long day. The coffee tasted delicious, and the piece of toast would carry him over until breakfast on the airplane. He ordered the UBER car online at 6:45 with an immediate return of 6:54 arrival at his front door. UBER was the best. He used it many times, and they never failed him. The drivers were polite with a smile on their face and ready to help loading luggage. He left his apartment and exited the front door just as the Lincoln Town Car pulled up to the curb. The interior had the smell of a fresh cleaning, and the driver handed him a small, cold bottle of water.

The airport was busy. Amazing, so many people departing at this early morning hour, he thought; business men and women. But, then again, the airport is busy all hours of the day. The 5-hour-and-5-minute flight was the one Aaron always preferred as it arrived in Charlotte Amalie about 3:30 with him in St. John for dinner.

He checked in, received his boarding pass, and proceeded to the TSA pre-check line. It was always fast and efficient for him. He arrived at the boarding gate and within a few minutes the agent announced boarding. He sent a text to Alphie advising him the flight was on time and he looked forward to seeing him. Alphie replied, *Hey boss, I'll be there. Vincent is sick today, so you're gonna have to put up with me.* Aaron smiled, turned his phone off, and put it in his breast pocket. The passengers boarded, and the flight was full. A woman sat down in the seat next to him.

"Good morning," she said.

Aaron greeted her and hoped she wasn't going to be a chatty-patty all the way to St. Thomas. She had on a bluish purple jumpsuit, lavender-colored glasses. Her nail polish was a lilac color and her lipstick mulberry orchid. Her lips looked like a bear's ass in a blueberry patch. I opened my morning paper, and she opened her book titled *How to be Happy in Life without Your Spouse.* Oh my God, I wasn't about to get into a conversation with this one.

The flight departed on time and Aaron was on his way. His thoughts turned to Maria. Wait 'til I tell her about Purple Priscilla sitting next to me. The crushing blow would have been if she were wearing Chanel No. 5. Underway and breakfast served, the flight attendant delighted him with a constant full coffee cup. Afterward, he leaned back and fell asleep. He woke up with the same flight attendant asking, with a smile, to put his seat in the full upright position.

Eleven

Landing in St. Thomas was always fun, as they arrived over the water with the mountains rising on the left side of the airplane. The runway was short with reversing and breaking intense.

Alfie met Aaron at the arrival area, reclaimed his case, and walked to the car a short distance in the lot.

"Good to see you, Doctor Aaron. How was the flight?"

"Good flight, and it's good to see you and be back home. You look great, Alfie! It's been a while since I've been here, but everything looks much the same," Aaron replied.

He always enjoyed being "home," as he often called it. At first, driving on the left side of the road in a car with a left-hand drive seemed confusing. The British left their mark. Alphie and Aaron talked all the way to the dock where they would board for the crossing to St. John. The drive to the ferry was about 35 minutes, with one just loading when they arrived. Alfie drove right on board.

"Davide Biagio heard you were coming today, courtesy of me, and is eager to see you again. He would like to have dinner with you tonight at The Estate."

"Great! How is Dave? I haven't communicated with him for about a month."

"He's good. I saw him yesterday; told him you were coming, and he said to have you call him right away. I'm sure he's waiting to hear from you."

Aaron took his iPhone out of his pocket and put in a call. Dave owns jewelry, fragrance, duty-free shops on King Street in the main part of the island. They've been friends for about 20 years. Dave and Aaron met in St. John at a tennis court, both looking for a partner. A beer and conversation after sealed their relationship like they had known each other all of their lives.

"Dave! Aaron."

"Hey, bud! It's good to hear from you. How ya been?"

"Fine, just fine. I just arrived and I'm on the ferry. I should be on the island by 5. Alphie says you wanted to meet for dinner at The Estate and I look forward to it."

"Great! How about seven?"

"You bet. See you at the bar. *We* have a lot to catch up on."

The crossing to St. John was beautiful. The afternoon air was like velvet: warm, low humidity, and just plain pleasant. The sun was noticeably intense. A nice break, however, from the hassles of the city.

Aaron arrived at the owner's suite, unpacked, took a shower to get rid of the airplane smell, and poured himself a Chivas. Delicious, he thought. He gained two hours. It's now 5:30, 10:30 p.m. in Milan, so he thought he'd send a message to Maria so she'd get it in the morning.

> *Buon Giorno, my beautiful lady! I arrived in St. John this afternoon in sunshine and warmth. The blue Caribbean sparkled as we approached the airport in St. Thomas. All I could think of is how much I would love to have you here with me. I am meeting and having dinner with a friend I have known for about 20 years. His name is Davide Biagio, and he is a person you would approve of, being Italian, but I will imagine it is you sitting across from me. I will write again soon. A presto! (See you soon.)*

Twelve

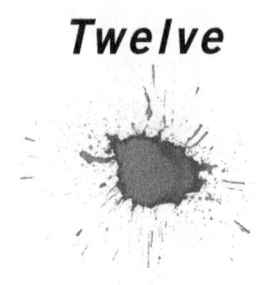

Alfie drove Aaron to The Estate around 6:45 p.m. He ordered his Chivas, rocks, twist, and just as he was being served, in walked Dave. They greeted each other with a firm handshake, a smile, and a pat on the back. Dave had those warm Italian looks with an olive skin, clean shaven, but a constant dark five-o'clock shadow. Dave's wife was visiting her family back home, so he was a first-class bachelor for a week.

"Great to see you," Aaron started.

"You too, it's been too long since you were here. How long ago was it?"

"Last spring, seems like yesterday. How's the wife, and I think your son and daughter are off to college. Am I correct?"

"Are you kidding? We're big-time empty nesters. Mark graduated from Rice in Houston, practicing law in Dallas. Stef finished at Northwestern, went to San Francisco, got a job in the home store at Williams-Sonoma because she studied graphic design."

They continued to talk about life, business, and Dave got around to Aaron's love life.

"Funny you should ask," Aaron replied. "I have much to tell you."

Aaron started to tell Dave about his time and relationship with Maria. He went into great detail about the twelve days they spent together. Finishing their drinks, they went to the dining room, sat down at the table, and ordered a fine Italian wine of Dave's choosing.

The dinner progressed, and Aaron finally said, "I don't know what I'm gonna do about this. Maria has expressed how she wishes Roberto were dead, and I do too, but it isn't going to happen any time soon, and I would never want to be guilty of murder or anything connected to it. I've never been in love with anyone before like I am with Maria. It's been a tough summer."

The conversation halted with the server asking how everything was.

"Everything is just fine," Dave responded.

Dave looked at Aaron, and the two looked at each other in total silence.

"I might be able to help you," Dave said with a slight smile on his face and slightly tipped head. The mood became even quieter. Aaron didn't know what to make of Dave's statement.

"What do you mean you could help me with that? What are you talking about?" Aaron asked.

"Well, it was just a thought but I do have some connections," Dave replied, waving his hand, brushing it off as frivolous conversation.

The meal, dessert, coffee, and cognac took about two hours. It was casual and comfortable. Aaron decided to pick up the tab, but Dave insisted on splitting the bill. They did and left the restaurant. Dave gave Aaron a ride, and they planned to meet in a couple of days for some tennis. Back at his villa, Aaron looked out on the moonlit Caribbean listening to the waves rush to the shore.

What did Dave mean by "I might be able to help you with this. I do have some connections."? He decided to pursue the question in a comical sort of way and find out. He sat down at his computer and sent a note to Maria. It would be 3:30 a.m. and she would now have two e-mails to read when she got up.

Come VA? How are you this morning? I had a wonderful evening with my longtime friend Davide Biagio. Drinks, dinner, dessert, coffee, and cognac. He's been on the island for about 30 years, having been born and raised in the Piemonte region of Italy, Pinerolo to be exact, about 60 miles southwest of Torino. His father owned a vineyard in the hills of Roletto, which his family owns, and is still producing fine wine. We met at a tennis court about 20 years ago each looking for a partner. We hit it off very well and have been friends ever since.

I thought of you all during the meal. The empty chair at our table was totally reserved for you. I hope you have a good day. We'll talk again soon. Love you; miss you!

Arrivederci!

Aaron brushed his teeth and crawled into bed.

Thirteen

Aaron woke at 8 a.m. He gained two hours coming down and had not adjusted. The first thing entering his mind was, "I might be able to help you." He took a shower, and after drying off, he pulled on clean underwear, a pair of shorts, and a T-shirt. His flip-flops felt good on his feet as he went to the office to grab a cup of coffee. Vincent was behind the desk on the telephone. He was finalizing a booking for November. He hung up and turned to Aaron.

"Hey, boss! Good to see you."

"Morning, Vinnie. Good to see you too. How ya feelin'?"

"Better! I'm sorry I couldn't make it to St. Thomas to pick you up but I had some bug lasting about 24 hours. I'm fine now."

"That's okay. I got here. Gotta run, I've got some e-mails to attend to. Later!"

Aaron rushed back to the villa to check his e-mail. Sure enough, one was from Maria. He settled back, sipped his coffee, and started reading.

Buon Giorno! I enjoyed your messages. I am sure it's a beautiful morning there. I looked up where you are, and it is certainly small. I'm also glad you have a friend who you enjoy. Be sure when you add the word "love" to the tennis score you are talking to me. Roberto has been a royal pain in the ass! He lost one client in late July; he has another ready to leave very soon. He has not been nice to me ever since I returned. If things don't change, something will. I wish he would just disappear for a while. I think of you often and hope we can meet sometime soon. Vieni a trovarmi! (Visit me soon.)

Maria

Finished, he sent an e-mail to Dave wanting to know if they could meet later in the day for some tennis. Dave almost immediately replied, saying he could get away about 4 o'clock, play a couple of sets, and after head to The Fatty Crab for some drinks and dinner. Aaron agreed as The Crab, as everyone called it, was one of his favorite places.

Aaron told Dave to come to the courts at his place and to bring some clean clothes. He could shower in the second bathroom at the villa.

After a 10-mile run, Aaron spent midday at the beach reading, walking, and swimming, thinking the exercise and activity would get his mind off the "help you" statement. It didn't work. The only accomplishment was the sunscreen Aaron frequently applied.

Dave arrived at Aaron's villa tennis court at a little after 4 p.m.

"Hey, guy! You ready to get whipped today?"

Aaron just smiled and said, "Tell you what! You take a number and have a seat. You're gonna need it, pal, cuz I'm gonna kick some butt!"

The games began, and Dave was surprised how fit Aaron was on the tennis court. He regularly played at the gym at home, so he was in great shape. Aaron wiped out Dave in two sets.

"You're an animal," Dave said, laughing. "You need to get married to slow you down."

"I wish I could," Aaron replied. "I would love to be married to Maria. I remember what you said last night: 'I can help you with that.'"

Silence fell, and each stared at the other. Dave knew he had opened Pandora's box, exposed a fuse, and Aaron wanted to light it.

They walked off the court and went to Aaron's villa to clean up. He poured them both a short Chivas while each went to his room to get dressed to go to The Crab.

Dave did not know what to think. Maybe he should do as Aaron advised, "take a number and have a seat." It had been a long time since he became involved in the family mishmash back in Italy, but he knew what and how to do it.

Fourteen

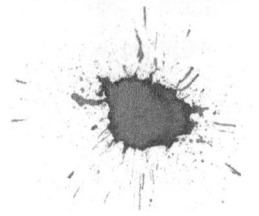

It was after 6:00 in the evening and The Crab was its usual busy place. Dave knew some of the people, as well as the management, and acknowledged them as they walked to the outdoor patio. The sun was low in the sky. The cool trade wind made the air comfortable. They sat down at a table for two by the railing offering a private conversation area. Aaron wanted to be alone with Dave and did not want anyone inviting themselves to their table. He was on a mission of information.

Scotch was in order, and they each decided on a Chivas on the rocks with a twist of lemon. The waiter brought the drinks and a menu for each. Asked if they wanted to hear about the specials, they politely said, "No."

They were in no hurry and talked about the tennis game, Aaron's staying in such good shape while leading the busy life of a physician. Yet, he still took time for exercise and yoga.

"Dave, we have known each other for a long, long time. You and your wife have been good friends, and I always look forward to seeing you both when I come to the island."

"I know," replied Dave. "Diane and I always enjoyed your coming down to visit. Will there be a rematch on the tennis court?"

"There will be if you can explain in detail what you said last night at dinner."

"What did I say?" asked Dave.

"I might be able to help you with that," replied Aaron. "What did you mean? It's about Roberto and Maria."

Dave had a look on his face as if to say, "I didn't want to go there;

me and my big mouth!" He sat looking out over the Caribbean and the darkening beautiful sunset. A cruise ship was departing the harbor, brilliantly lit with its running lights on — a beautiful sight. Dave wished he were on it.

Silence lasted for at least a minute as Dave continued to look out over the sea, the departing cruise ship, and the setting sun. He turned his head, looked at a staring Aaron in the face, took in a deep breath, pursed his lips, let out a long sigh, and said, "All right. I will tell you. It's a long, complicated process, but in the end Roberto will disappear."

"Disappear?" asked Aaron, cocking his head and widening his eyes and came closer to hear. "What do you mean by 'disappear'?"

Dave looked at Aaron and said slowly, "No one on this side of the world will know anything about his disappearance. Let's just call it 'vaporization'."

Suddenly, the conversation took on a whispering tone.

"So how does this take place? What...what...I...I don't understand? What are you talking about? Murder?"

"You will never know," Dave said slowly with a slight smirk on his face. He continued, "The day will come when he will no longer be here or there or anywhere. Trust me. I know how it's done and who to contact. Roberto will go 'on vacation'."

Aaron had a chill come over his body. All he said was, "Dave!" *Is this for real?* he thought. His head was spinning, and as he slowly moved it side to side he said distinctly, "I am not going to involve myself in any murder, extermination, liquidation, or vaporization, as you said."

"You won't. It will all be done without your being there. The only thing involved on your side of the pond is your checkbook."

Aaron sat in a state of unbelievable and incomprehensible information. His years with Dave had always been so enjoyable. *Here he is telling me about a person disappearing, and I don't know what to think.* His head was in a state of twisting and turning. After a minute or so, he calmed down with his curiosity piqued.

"Tell me more. I wanna know what you mean by everything you have said."

The server came over, and they ordered another round of scotch, letting him know they were in no hurry and would order after the next round.

The second round of drinks finished, the server came over and took their orders. Aaron could hardly believe what Dave had been saying, and he just couldn't decide on his evening meal. Finally, he ordered the stone crab cakes.

Dave looked at Aaron. "First of all, this conversation never took place. Do you agree?"

"Yes," replied Aaron.

"You have to give me your word you will never disclose any information I am going to give you. My name is never mentioned. Do you promise?"

"You have my word. I will never disclose anything. This night never took place," Aaron said with a somewhat forced grin on his face while moving his head side to side. He didn't know what else to do.

"OK, my friend, I trust you." They shook hands. Just then the server came with their meals.

"Let's eat and go back to your place," Dave said. Aaron forced a smile and nodded in the affirmative.

Fifteen

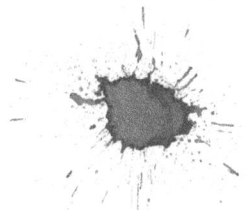

It was a quiet ride to Aaron's villa. Dave drove and didn't have much to say. They arrived about 8:30.

"Would you like a glass of port?" Aaron asked.

"Yes, sounds good after that delicious meal."

"Let's go out on the patio. It's nice with the sound of the waves rolling up on the beach."

"You ever been here during a hurricane?" Dave asked.

"No, I haven't had the pleasure, but I've had damage reports from Vinnie. Luckily, they haven't been as bad as some have had around here."

Aaron wanted to get right to the point and wasn't interested in meteorology, but he sensed Dave might be attempting to dissolve the issue.

"Sit down and get comfortable," Aaron inviting his hand toward the chair where Dave would relax.

They sat down, clinked their glasses together, and Aaron looked at Dave as if to say, "OK, let's hear about it," but it didn't come out.

After what seemed a long silence, and Aaron not asking, Dave started.

"I was born in Roletto, Italy. My family owned a vineyard in the hills near the town. My grandfather started it. They produced mostly white wines of the Gavi variety. They're still doing so today. My father is 74 and served in the Italian Army. He and my mother, of the same age, have lived on the estate all of their lives, raised my two sisters and one brother. I am the only one who left Italy. My dad still goes to work at the winery every day. He has a great staff and dedicated workers."

Dave stopped momentarily, and Aaron thought, it's all very interesting, but where is he going with all of this? They both took a sip of their port.

Dave continued:

"When my father was in the military, his unit became known as The Legion. They were a large group of fighters, same as the Seals in the U.S. Navy. They did secretive missions all over Italy, France, and Germany. They became known as 'The Legionnaires'; you didn't mess with them. After the war ended, some difficult times evolved with the Italian mafia seemingly very interested in the wine business, especially our wine business, and they needed to be stopped. My father invited a couple of his Legionnaires to the estate and discussed what to do to halt this creeping and edging in of this group apparently from Sicily. This infiltration continued for about eight months to a year, I am told, as I was not yet born. It was a challenge to my dad and our entire family."

Aaron sat mesmerized with the information Dave was giving to him. How did he know all this?

"My father had a couple of his buddies take control of anyone who started to become extensively interested in our wine business. Then one day one of the mafiosi disappeared. To this day no one knows what happened to him. One of the Legionnaires moved to the United States. I know him well.

"So is this how it would happen? Is this the course I would be taking to make Roberto disappear? What do they do? How does it happen?" Aaron asked.

Dave looked at Aaron, made a gesture with his head, and passed the palm of his hand upward and toward the beach. "You will never know. It will just happen."

"So where does it go from here?" Aaron asked.

"If you decide to go through with it, just contact me. I'll tell you where you have to go to start the process. You will work through my contact."

It was now 11:30 and both were getting tired because the conversation was slowing, and silence became evident. They finished their port some time ago, so Aaron stood up. Dave followed as they both went to the bar and left their glasses. Aaron walked out with Dave to the car.

"Wanna do something tomorrow? Lunch, tennis, or whatever," Aaron asked.

"I can't. We have a large shipment coming in the morning via cargo ship, so I'll have to be there and here to inventory it all. It ends up as an all-day process. I'll be in touch. Diane comes back on Saturday afternoon and then, 'The Party's Over,'" with Dave singing the words to the music. They both laughed.

"Not for me," Aaron responded. "Let's talk Friday."

Dave drove away and Aaron went inside to the computer. A message to Maria was the next duty on his mind.

Buon Giorno! I'm writing late as I have had a long and interesting day. I went for a good run this morning and then spent time at the beach in front of the villa. It was a beautiful day today. I met Dave about 4:00 for a game of tennis. I beat his posterior, as you have referred to it, big time. I think he was surprised. We showered here, changed clothes, then headed to a favorite bar called The Fatty Crab. Good place right on the sea. We had a good talk and a port back at the villa. Dave's wife Diane is out of town and will be back Saturday. I have only two more days here and then back to the grind. Hope all is well with you and Roberto has calmed down. Love you and miss you. I wish you were here. Gotta catch some sleep. Love you! Miss you!

Sixteen

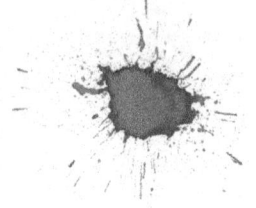

Aaron woke. It was still dark out. He looked at his watch with the Indiglo nightlight. It was just after 2 a.m. He tossed and turned to his other side, but it didn't relieve him of the conversation he'd had with Dave last evening. His thoughts became saturated about getting involved with the disappearance of a person. He could not figure out or grasp how all this would take place. He could not go back to sleep, so he got up and went to his computer. As he'd expected, a morning message from Maria.

Good morning, my love. Oh! How I wish you were here. I am so lonely and disgusted with Roberto, his attitude and demeanor. We decided, or I should say, Roberto decided to go to Portofino for a week. He has lost his second client which he depended on for a large income, and he is constantly complaining about everything. He said WE needed a break. He called me a "bitch" the other day and told me to get out of his sight for the rest of the day. I ended up crying and finding myself lonely and alone. I was so hurt. He apologized, but I felt he didn't mean it. I know I said he needed me, but I am beginning to stop and think, does he in reality need me? I'm considering just being alone in Milan for a few days. Would you be able to come and be with me? We could have such a fun time. I know the city well. We would be very local. My favorite hotel in Milan is the Spadari al Duomo. It's in the center of the city within walking distance to The Galleria, The Duomo, and The Teatro alla Scala. Do you like opera? The hotel staff at Spadari always treats us, or me if I am alone, very nice. Think about it as I am always thinking about you. I hope your day goes better than mine. I detest getting in bed next to him. Love you. — I am crying!

Aaron felt lonely, and he could do nothing about it. Go to Milan? He realized he couldn't. He had already spent the past week in St. John and he had backed up his patients over a week or so. I have to return home, he thought. I must go forward to work. He went back to bed and lay on his back. When he opened his eyes, it was light out, and the clock read 9:22 a.m.

Coffee! The order of the day, so he went to the office.

"Hey, good morning, boss!" Vinnie said. "You're up late."

"I know. I had a late night and woke up for a few hours; couldn't sleep. Say, can you get me to the airport in St. Thomas Saturday? My flight leaves at 2:30."

"Sure. I'll take care of it. We'll plan to take the 10 o'clock ferry. It will give you plenty of time to get through customs and immigration. It's always packed on Saturday."

"Perfect," Aaron replied. "I'll be ready to go at 9:30."

"Oh, and good news," Vinnie said. "I have a new reservation for the owner's suite for the next two weeks arriving this coming Sunday."

"Hey, great!" Aaron said, pleased, but he kept thinking about Maria and walked slowly back to his villa. A run would be the next order of the day around noon, he thought.

A coffee and a sports drink gave Aaron a boost, making him ready for a good 10- to 12-mile run. Every step of the way he thought about the situation his life was presenting to him. He started to run a little faster. The air was still cool. He clenched his fists and teeth thinking about that jerk, Roberto. He'd always thought Italian men treated women with the utmost respect. When he returned all hot and sweaty, he felt better and ready for a good shower. He saw the light on his cell phone illuminated, alerting him someone had called. He picked it up. It was Dave. He listened to the voicemail.

"Aaron? Dave! Let's plan on going tomorrow afternoon around 4:00. I'll pick you up. We'll plan on a farewell dinner at The Chateau de Bordeaux. I'll make a dinner reservation for 7:00. Haven't been there for some time, but I understand they changed the menu, and it's quite good. If it's not gonna work, call me back. Otherwise, I'll see you at 4:00."

Good, Aaron thought. The rest of the day was going to be R & R with reading if he could get his mind to it.

He sat down to his computer and sent a message to Maria.

Maria. I am so sorry for what's happening to you. Roberto should not treat you like that. You don't deserve it and it answers the question quite clearly as to whether or not you need him or he needs you. He doesn't, and you don't.

I read your horoscope today, and it said, "Fearless courage isn't courage; it's foolishness! Real courage always has a fear attached to it. Life is better when you make room in your mind for fear to leave and excitement to begin."

Think about it! I have to go now but will be in touch later.

Aaron

Seventeen

Aaron spent the rest of the day on the patio. Even though he didn't go out into the sun, he wore sunscreen, as he knew the reflection off the water could cause sunburn. He read some of the latest articles from the *Journal of the American Dermatology Association* (*JMDA*). He knew he had to get back to work as he had patients waiting for him.

Around 3:15, he shaved, showered again, and dressed for dinner.

Dave pulled up promptly at 4:00 and they left for The Chateau de Bordeaux cocktail lounge before dinner. Dave talked about the shipment arriving. It wasn't as large as he had expected, so it didn't take as much time as before.

Aaron got right to the point: "What if I decided to go through with this…I guess I call it 'an elimination of Roberto'?"

"You call me and I'll refer you to The Contact up north. He will be in touch with you. He will never reveal his name. You will never know his name. He will always be known to you as 'The Contact.' He does not live where you do. He will tell you all, and everything you need to do. When and if you do contact me, use the code word 'Milan' and I will know what we're talking about. Never say 'Roberto' or 'Maria' and do not call me once you speak to him. From then on, the ball is in your court. When he contacts you, he will say, 'I'm calling about your trip to Milan.' Once this happens, I am out of it and the conversation never happened. OK?"

Aaron, mesmerized, thought how well planned, organized, and clean it would become once the connection was made. Would there be no trace? It was as if Dave had done this before. He didn't ask; maybe he had.

The maître d' came and advised their table was ready any time they wished to be served. They finished their scotch and a few minutes later proceeded to the dining room. The atmosphere was very pleasant; the menu diverse with seafood as the main appetizer and entree. Aaron ordered the chef's salad with anchovies followed by the garlic sautéed prawns and rice. The conversation never went back to "Milan" but centered on Aaron getting back to work and when he would be down again. Dave talked about his success in St. John, and he would probably never leave.

"Want a port?" Aaron asked when they were leaving.

"I can't," Dave replied. "With Diane coming home tomorrow, I have some cleaning up to do."

Eighteen

Morning came, and Aaron had his case packed and ready to go by 9:30. Vinnie drove the van over to his villa and loaded the bag.

"Only one?" Vinnie asked with a smile, gesturing his hands like a beggar.

"Yup, I travel light. Everything I need is in one bag."

Arrival at the dock took about ten minutes, and the ferry from St. Thomas was just arriving. After a short wait, they drove on and it departed at exactly 10 a.m. The 40-minute ride was quiet with Aaron on the deck looking at St. John as it disappeared in the distance.

The drive to the airport was no problem. It was just the usual traffic. Checking in at the airline desk was also quick with his preassigned favorite seat, 2A. He proceeded to immigration and customs. He always thought this was nonsense as St. Thomas and St. John were both U.S. possessions and United States currency is used. The line was long with no provision for TSA pre-check or first-class passengers. You could sense they couldn't give a crap about anyone being late or even missing a flight. You were all one and the same. After about 50 minutes, he cleared everything and was ready for a quick bite to eat before departing. No, I don't think I will, he thought. I'll be fed on the airplane. Just then, another thought flashed in his mind.

He went to duty-free. He had a plan for some time and decided to follow through with it now. He bought a one-quarter ounce bottle of Chanel No. 5 perfume. He would take it home, put a drop or two every day or so on a special piece of linen on his bed stand. He would always think of Maria and wake up to her scent.

The flight boarded and departed on time. Leaving St. Thomas requires a steep climb and a right turn out to avoid terra firma, better known as the mountains. He always enjoyed the departure. About two to three minutes later, it would be all water most of the way home.

Arriving at his destination, he found the terminal busy as usual. He called the UBER car and one arrived in about 11 minutes. He opened the door to his apartment and found the mail on the entrance table. The door attendant always took good care of everything while Aaron was gone. Nothing appeared new in the mail except the usual Visa bill, utilities, advertising, and catalogs, catalogs, catalogs.

It was Saturday, so Aaron called the office and left a message to let them know he was back. He would be in early Monday morning to find out what his schedule was like the rest of the week. He would be awake about two hours early and probably arrive before they heard the message, but he thought it best to leave it anyway.

He unpacked, put his soiled clothes in the washer, packed his trousers, shorts, and some long-sleeved shirts ready to drop off on Monday morning at the local laundry on his way to the bus.

It wasn't very late, and because he'd gained a couple of hours coming home, he put on his coat and trotted off to Jake's for a nightcap. He took his iPad Mini with him to write a note to Maria. He did want to get to bed early to catch up on the time-zone change.

Entering Jake's, he immediately smiled with the quietness of the place on a Saturday evening. He headed over to his usual table. Max was not working, but instead, a female bartender he had not seen before. She was very nice looking and pleasant; she came over to his table and asked what he would like. His Chivas, rocks, twist arrived, and he settled down to write to Maria.

Maria, my darling. I just arrived home from my week in St. John. I have to get back to work on Monday morning. I've been thinking of you quite a bit. Your thought of coming to Milan is intriguing. Sadly, I cannot. I have taken too much time off already. It's chilly here, and winter will be arriving soon. Have you any plans to come back again? I am at Jake's enjoying my libation and looking at the table where you usually sit. It's not occupied right now. The place is nice and quiet. It's good to be here to end the day before I go home and go to bed. I have to tell you: I bought a bottle of Chanel No. 5 at duty-free in St. Thomas before departure. I'm going to put a couple of drops on a linen handkerchief and keep it on my bed stand to remind me of you. Wish you were here.

Love you and looking forward,
Aaron

The walk back to the apartment seemed lonely. I'm tired of being alone in my life, Aaron thought. All my friends are now married with families. I would like to do the same. I've always desired the companionship of a wife. It's never worked out, and his thoughts turned to Dave and the Milan project. I have never engaged in any illegal activity, let alone eliminating someone. I know of some drugs that would take care of the problem with another person, but to have it done in a covert, stealthy manner without my doing anything would be simple. He readied himself for bed and decided he would go to the office early tomorrow morning for a quick review of his patients records and find out his schedule.

Nineteen

Aaron woke up early with his body rhythm working on the time zone in the Caribbean. He would have to go to bed later tonight to try to catch up. He went to his computer. There was an e-mail from Maria.

> *Oh Aaron! This has been a terrible day. Roberto was so angry with me for no apparent reason. We usually go to the same restaurant for breakfast after Sunday morning mass and he told me he didn't want to be with me and walked away. I felt so lonely and rejected. He didn't speak to me all day. His losing the clients has made him, how do you say it, an ass? I don't know how much longer I am going to be able to take this. You are constantly on my mind. I am heading to Milan for a couple of days. Wish you were here.*
>
> *Love you,*
> *Maria*

It was Sunday morning and Aaron felt perplexed. He changed into his running gear and left the apartment toward the river. He didn't know what to think except Roberto had to go, but how? *Maybe I should call Dave about the Milan project*. He continued his run with his heart pounding, probably more from Maria's e-mail than the exercise. *I could call him just to see what it entails*. With a shower and breakfast finished, he went to the clinic to do some work. Just before leaving at noon, he decided to give Dave a call. It would be 2 p.m. there and being Sunday

Dave might not be home. He thought he'd try anyway. He could always leave a message.

The phone rang; Diane answered.

"Hi Diane, it's Aaron."

"Well hello, it's so good to hear your voice. I understand you two had an eventful week while I was up north."

"We did. It's been a long time. We played tennis, at which I beat him handily."

"I heard. I think he enjoyed it, however. He told me he let you beat him."

"Yeah, dream on. I have to say he made me earn it. It was fun and we had good days at several clubs and nice dinners. I'm sorry I missed you. Is he there?"

"I missed seeing you. He is here. I'll get him for you."

Aaron could hear Diane in the background calling Dave and could hear his footsteps as he came to the phone.

"Hey, guy," Dave said. "How ya doin'? You back in the groove of things?"

"Just about. I woke up early this morning, went for a run, came back, cleaned up, had some breakfast, came to the clinic to get ready for tomorrow."

"I sure enjoyed seeing you this past week and everything we did. I hope you'll plan to get down here again soon so I can whip your butt in a tennis match. Actually, as Diane said, I let you win. Any plans?"

"Yeah right, you let me win. No plans, but what I wanted to talk to you about is my upcoming trip to Milan."

Dave didn't hesitate but knew what Aaron had in mind.

"I think it best to hook you up with an expert. Why don't I get ahold of him? He'll contact you and give you all the information you'll need. I'll let him handle it from here on."

"OK, any idea when he might contact me?"

"No, but he will fairly soon. Just be patient. He'll give you all the info you'll need."

"Thanks, Dave. We'll talk again, but I won't let you in on anything about Milan."

"Deal, buddy! Be good and take care."

"You bet. Take care."

They hung up and the understanding between them clear.

Twenty

The next morning came early but later than the day before, so it seemed. He shaved, showered, dressed, and put on a clean-starched shirt and tie. He dropped off his laundry at the cleaners on his way to the bus. The cleaners opened at 6:00 and had the motto "*in before 8, out by 2*." He could pick them up on his way home. The bus arrived right on time at 6:21 and the driver said, "Hey, Mr. Aaron. I've missed you. Been out of town?"

"Yes. I went to my vacation home on St. John in the Virgin Islands. It was good to get some warmth for a change. You drivin' an earlier schedule?"

"No, I just go back and start all over again. I'll be at this stop again at 7."

"Well, good to see you back." Aaron took his seat and opened the morning paper. Nothing new; just the same old stuff.

He left the bus at his usual stop. It was about 6:40 and no one came to the office much before 7. His first patient would be arriving at 8:00. He would have a full, busy day. The sun had been good for his career, and the summer rays provided more clients, shall we say, coming in for removal of their rewards for basking at the beach.

The week went by with the customary routine. He heard from Maria on a morning daily basis and he responded before he went to bed at night. The sounds of her messages were grim, almost to the point of heartbreaking. Aaron would always respond with an encouraging word expressing the best was yet to come.

He had not heard from his contact person and a week had gone by.

He thought it would be immediate, but it did not happen. He knew he could not call Dave because their understanding was not to do so once they had made contact with each other concerning Milan.

Aaron made his trips to Jake's, saw Max, made small talk with some of the regulars. He still liked going to the gym on Friday afternoons and headed home afterward. His latest e-mails from Maria told him she was in Milan, resting, shopping, and just enjoying her time away from Roberto. He was going to join her for the next weekend, but she was skeptical of what would take place. Aaron always responded. He wished he could be with her, but at this point it would be impossible.

This Friday he came home early and decided to fix a light supper and spend a quiet evening. He poured himself a scotch, went out on the patio to enjoy the cool air and think.

Twenty-One

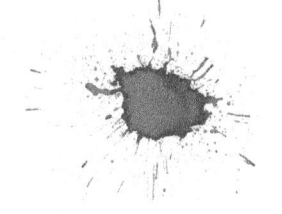

The phone broke the silence.

He walked in from the patio and put his drink down. The caller I.D. on his landline read *"Private Number Unknown Name."* He usually didn't answer these calls but thought it might be the one. He answered.

"Hello, this is Aaron." There was a delayed silence on the other end. Aaron thought it might be a solicitation call and was about to hang up when the voice took in a deep breath. "Hello. I am calling in regards to your inquiry about your interest in 'Milan.'" The voice was deep and masculine. Aaron hesitated. A rush went through his body, and his heart started beating faster. He could feel a flushing in his face and neck.

"Yes, thank you for calling. I would very much like to talk to you about 'Milan' and see what I could learn about it. I've never been in the city so I'm interested in meeting with someone who could help me."

"I think you would like it very much and most assuredly be very happy with the results. I can arrange everything for you. You won't have to lift a finger." The voice was businesslike, pleasant, and gave Aaron a good feeling although he was reluctant to engage in the project. "We must meet to talk about the trip in which you are interested."

"Fine. Where would you like to meet? I live in the city close to the Belmont Hotel."

"Yes, I know where you live," the voice said. "There's a Starbucks around the corner from the Belmont. We need to meet tomorrow morning at 9:30."

"Tomorrow is Saturday and I am free. How will I know you?"

"You don't need to know me. You will never know me. All you need to know about me is, I am The Contact. I will recognize you by what you are wearing, which is?"

Aaron thought for a moment.

"I'll have on jeans, a red shirt, and a tan baseball cap with the logo '*St. John VI*' on the front. I'll choose a comfortable table near the back, close to the exit. I'll arrive promptly at 9:30."

"I will find you. If I'm not there at that time, don't panic. I will be there shortly."

He hung up abruptly without Aaron being able to say anything. He put the phone down and cupped his hands to his face. What am I getting myself into? he thought. He stayed in a sitting position for a minute or so, took in a deep breath, placed his hands on top of his head, looked toward the ceiling, and let out a loud sigh. This is not good, but appears clandestine. Nevertheless, he could go and listen. He could call it off before it ever begins.

He went to the Pizza Hut down the street and ordered a small with everything. Finished, he walked along the river. The horn blew loudly. He jumped. There was no warning. He was so deep in thought he almost became a statistic by crossing the street without looking. The driver said, "Watch where the fuck you're going," and flipped him the middle finger. Aaron raised his right hand, pressed his index, second, and third fingers together, saying loudly, "Read between the lines."

When he arrived at the apartment, he did not turn on any lights. He often would sit in the dark, as he loved the peace, the night lights, the relaxation and thought. He fixed a glass of port, went out to the patio and sat. His thoughts turned to Maria and the conversation he'd had earlier with whom he referred to as The Contact. He put the coffee on in the automatic mode for morning.

TIL DEATH DO US PART • 61

Finishing his port, even though he was not tired, Aaron decided to write to Maria and go to bed. It surprised him to see her e-mail in the inbox. He opened it.

Aaron, my love, Buon Giorno! It was so good to read your e-mail of last night. It's Sunday morning here, and Roberto and I went to mass, grabbed a light continental breakfast with a delicious cappuccino. He's been so distant from me. I don't feel accepted by him anymore. I sense he doesn't love me anymore. I feel I'm in the way, just walking aimlessly about with no purpose. This has to change. After we had returned home, he said he had to go to his office for a couple of hours. I felt it was just to get away from me. So I went walking down via Corso Buenos Aires, a famous shopping street in Milan. Stores are not open on Sunday in Italy, but some coffee and pastry shops are. I came upon a window where I stopped for a moment. Suddenly, in the reflection of the glass I thought I saw Roberto's car. I turned, and it was. What was it doing here? We live at Via Giovanni Batista Pergolesi 1224 and I was just a few blocks from our flat. This is residential. His office is not in this neighborhood. I went into the coffee shop next to where I was with a clear view of his car. After a couple of cappuccinos, I saw Roberto coming out of a doorway with descending steps from some upstairs flats. He was with a woman. They stopped for a moment, hugged, kissed passionately, and Roberto got into the car waving at her and drove off. She returned to the flat. Aaron, he is having an ongoing affair. Now I know why he's gone in the afternoons two to three times a week. We are — or should I say were? — planning to go to Portofino next month for the entire 30 days. Unless he changes plans, I will go just to see what happens. As far as I am concerned, I am through with him. The 30 days would give me time to think things through. I don't know what to do! Where do I go with this? He spoke of coming to the U.S. sometime soon, and if he makes plans, I will surely be there as well. I hope you have a good day with your new friend. HELP me!

Love you too, and miss you too,
Maria

Aaron replied:

I have a plan. Just sit tight and be patient; more later.

Love you, Aaron

Twenty-Two

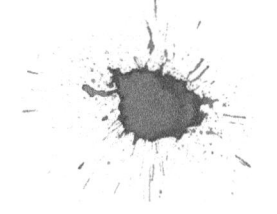

Aaron opened his eyes as the sun was just about to rise above the horizon. It was 7:12 a.m. The sky was clear and forecasted to be a sunny day with a high in the 60's. He felt fine even though he did not sleep well. He decided to get up, have a cup of coffee, and go out for a run. Even though the temperature was 42°, it didn't bother him as he had jogged in much colder temperatures before. He had a good run and his body seemed to awaken. An hour later he was back home.

The shower felt good and very cleansing. He didn't shave because this was his day off. He pulled on his underwear, jeans, T-shirt, red shirt, his shoes and socks. He was ready to go. A little cereal filled the stomach. It was now 9:15 and a five-minute walk to Starbucks. He grabbed his cap and Ray-Ban sunglasses.

Saturday morning at Starbucks was usually busy and proved to be the same this morning. He ordered a decaf coffee, a muffin, and took a seat in the rear of the coffee shop. He had a plain view of the front door. 9:30 came and no one entered. About 9:45 a man came in, seemed uninterested in anyone, and went to the counter to order. Close behind was a young couple engaged in laughter and conversation followed by a man who had his morning paper under his arm. The first man picked up his coffee and a croissant and immediately came to Aaron. No handshake or acknowledgment offered. He was wearing jeans, a light-colored shirt, cowboy boots, and, of course, a red baseball cap and sunglasses. He was a large man, not fat, rough hands, and appeared to work in construction. Aaron noticed the ruddy complexion and tanned skin. I could do a lot for him in my clinic, he thought.

The Contact started the conversation.

"When you order a croissant you'd think they'd give you more butter. I asked for it but the barista said, 'come back if you need more,' and I know I will. Excuse me while I have to go back and get more," the man grumbled as he waved down an employee cleaning up and asked him to bring him more butter. After a minute, it appeared. In the meantime, neither Aaron nor The Contact spoke a word.

"So, you're interested to know more about Milan," he spoke softly. Other customers were around them, but the table was adjacent to the glass window so it gave them some privacy. "Are you still interested?"

Aaron thought for a moment and decided to say, "Yes, I am. Are we going to discuss the itinerary?"

"No," replied The Contact. "This was just to see if you would show up. Here is what you have to do to get a complete itinerary. There will be no misunderstanding. I'm only going to say this once so listen to me carefully.

"You must book a room at The Belmont for tomorrow. Check-in is at 3 p.m. or later. You will check in and I will meet you in the lobby by the elevators. I will be wearing what I am wearing right now. We will go to your room to discuss the outline leading you to your Milan setup. You will check in at 3:30 p.m. and not before. I will arrive promptly at 3:30, this time, promptly. You will not enter the room before I meet you. We will enter together at the same time. You will bring with you $10,000 in cash in your blue Nike gym bag; I know you have more than one. This is to secure your interest and commitment. It is my fee for the work I have done, and will do, to complete the contract. You just said you were interested, which is a commitment. If you do not show, I will come after you. I know where you live, what work you do, the car you drive, the gym you go to, and the bar you frequent. You will not waste my time as it will not be pretty if you do, and I will not waste your time." He spoke with a firm clear voice, no gestures, just an either/or attitude. "Do you understand...Doctor?"

Aaron was surprised with the knowledge The Contact knew. How did he learn about me?

"Yes, I understand."

The Contact got up, did not say a word, took his coffee, and abruptly went out through the door to his left and disappeared down the street.

Aaron finished his coffee and knew he had to get to the bank. It closed at 1:00 p.m. He kept a stash of cash in his safe-deposit box in $100 bills. He rented the largest box available. Every month, he deposited in the box at least $2,000 in cash. It was for his investments in St. Thomas and St. John when needed. He knew he had enough in the box to secure the $10,000. He had to go back to the apartment to get the described gym bag. He did have several of them. Arriving at the bank, he went to the basement, signed in, presented his ID, and went with the bank employee to the caged area locating his box number 6859. He removed the box, took a room, and opened it. It was neatly organized with enough cash to satisfy The Contact's request. The currency, wrapped with a $100 band totaling $1,000 in each band. He filled the gym bag with ten bundles, left the room, waited for the clerk to take him back to his lockbox. Aaron left the bank with the gym bag, no heavier than one containing his gym gear, and went home. He called The Belmont and made a reservation for the next day. He could only get a junior suite two-room accommodation for $435/night plus taxes. He booked the room.

Maria — Good morning. I read your last e-mail several times and I am just sick the way you are being treated. This, I think, will all change soon. Like I said, I have a plan. It's been quite a day; too much to explain. Beautiful weather here. Since I arrived back from St. John, it's been busy trying to catch up with all my work. I've been to Jake's a couple of nights this week and have seen you sitting at your normal table. It's a perfect spot for you and I wish you could come back here to be there. It's late, and I must get to bed. I plan to get up early, go for a run, have an early lunch, and then am meeting with a friend I just met around 3:30. I'll see you in my dreams with the scent of Chanel.

Twenty-Three

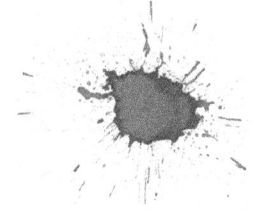

It was 8:15 a.m. on a sunny Sunday morning and Aaron thought he should get going. He needed his run first thing if he was going to do it. Today would be a busy day. He wondered if what he was doing this afternoon was very smart. He never involved himself in sneaky, underground activities. He felt strongly about getting Maria out of her environment and having happier times.

The run went well as usual, and he felt better and exhilarated. It was time for lunch, so he went to La Pronto, a restaurant a few blocks away — Italian to celebrate. The rest of the early hours of the afternoon, he spent watching football. It was now 3:15 so he thought he'd better get going. He was already in his jeans, red shirt, St. John baseball cap, and Ray-Bans. He grabbed the gym bag and left the apartment.

He walked briskly to The Belmont, arriving at 3:28. The check-in desk had two people ahead of him. He looked over toward the elevator but did not see The Contact. The desk clerk, however, recognized his address.

"You live just a few blocks from here."

"I know. I am having my apartment painted today, and the smell is quite strong, so I thought it best I just take the night off, relax here, and watch some football. I'll check out in the morning, go back to the apartment, change clothes, and head for work."

"Sounds good," the clerk replied.

He must think I'm here for a one-night stand. Dream on, pal.

Aaron presented the clerk his credit card and driver's license, took his key, picked up the bag, and headed toward the elevator. Just as he was about to enter where the elevators were located, The Contact appeared out of nowhere from somewhere carrying the same gym bag as Aaron's.

"Glad to see you're on time. You take directions very well," The Contact said.

Aaron said nothing; still no handshake, no smile, just beady eye contact.

They went into the elevator, and the door closed with two other people entering with them. The couple departed on the 5th floor. Aaron's room was on the 9th. The Contact took the gym bag Aaron brought and gave him an identical bag he'd brought. Nothing was said until they arrived at room 928. Aaron put the key card in the lock and the green light illuminated. He twisted the knob and entered, observing very nicely appointed mini-suite accommodations. The Contact followed, grabbed the "do not disturb" sign, placing it on the doorknob outside. He entered, closed the door, latched the lock, took the security chain and slid it in place. Aaron was a good six feet away from him. He turned around and faced The Contact.

"OK," The Contact said. "Let's get started. Take off your clothes; all of them." He spoke slowly, distinctly, and he meant it.

Aaron froze. His face became gawky and wide-eyed with his mouth opening. At least seven to ten seconds passed with Aaron starting to shake his head.

"What the fuck are you asking me to do? I didn't come here to have sex with you. I don't do that shit!" Aaron was visibly shaken.

The Contact remained unruffled, didn't raise his voice but spoke calmly and with firmness.

"Don't flatter yourself, Doctor. I didn't come here to have sex with anyone. If I did, I would do it with a much better-looking guy and better built than you. Now take off all, and I mean all, of your clothes."

"That's enough," Aaron said. "Give me the bag back. I'm out of here."

Aaron started toward the door and The Contact pushed him back.

"You're in this now, and there's no escape. By my taking the gym bag, you've made a down payment, even though I haven't counted it, it's now mine. Now I'm gonna tell you again for the last time: Take off all of your clothes including your underwear!"

"No, I am not," Aaron firmly said. "I want out!"

"Didn't you hear me? I said 'no escape.' If you do not comply with my instructions, I will have no choice but to go to the front desk and report you for inviting me to your hotel room for a sexual encounter. They know you live very close to here, and why would a guy rent a room for one night? The police will be notified, they will have your name, I will tell them everything, and you will be destroyed personally and professionally."

"Who would believe you?"

"I have the money you gave me. I wouldn't show it all to them, but a couple of hundred-dollar bills would be convincing. Besides, I have witnesses."

"You asshole! What are you talking about — 'witnesses'?"

The Contact produced a picture of the two of them at Starbucks. Aaron had his hand on the Contact's hand. He gave it to Aaron.

He took the picture, looked at it. His eyes widened; he clenched his jaw, took in a deep breath, and said, "Where did you get this? Who took it?"

"Do you remember when I entered Starbucks, and a young couple came in behind me? Then a man with a newspaper under his arm entered after them. They all work for me, and they took several pictures. This is not the only one. Now…take…off…your…clothes! Throw them over to me!"

Aaron suddenly realized he was in deep kimchi. There was no escape. He thought of his reputation ruined, his profession gone, imploding everything he'd worked for in life. He thought of Maria and what she was going through. This is nothing. "All right, you've got me," Aaron surrendered. "I will comply with your demand, but you have to promise me you will not, and I mean you will never, divulge this to anyone."

"You have my word. I will tell no one, and when I say you have my word, you have my word."

Aaron made him repeat his promise slowly. The Contact did. Aaron put out his hand and The Contact reluctantly put out his. The understanding was now sealed by the handshake.

Aaron proceeded to remove his baseball cap and glasses, his shirt and T-shirt, and threw them to him. His cell phone fell out of his shirt pocket. He picked it up and gave it to him. He hesitated, and The Contact gestured down with the first finger of his left hand to remove the rest. Aaron shook his head in disgust, took off his shoes and socks, loosened his belt, unzipped his jeans, and dropped them to the floor and stepped out of them. He tossed them to The Contact. He stood in his underwear.

The Contact said, "OK. You can leave your shorts on. I'm convinced you're not wired." He told Aaron to open the gym bag he brought and take out a pair of gym shorts and a T-shirt and said, "Put them on. Now we can talk."

Aaron slipped into the shorts, put the T-shirt on, sat down in a chair behind him, and stared at The Contact. This is disgusting but all he could think of was Maria and what she would be doing now. He realized she was probably in bed. It was 11 p.m. in Milan.

The Contact sat down on the sofa next to him, picked up the gym bag Aaron had brought, unzipped it, looked inside, and saw wrappers of $100 bills. He thumbed through each one, counting them. It was all there. He took out a pad of paper and a pencil. Aaron sat down in a chair behind him.

Twenty-Four

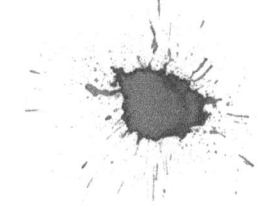

The Contact started the conversation. "Tell me about this person in Milan."

"Let's play this game fair and square! You take off all your clothes! How do I know you're not wired?" Aaron was adamant. He resented the attitude of The Contact, so he decided to throw it right back into his face.

"Well, you don't," The Contact replied. "Tell me where this person lives, where they shop, drive, go to church, buy groceries, vacation, everything about them."

"Take your clothes off like you made me do!" Aaron said firmly. "And I mean it!"

"I don't think you are in a position to tell me what to do," The Contact replied.

Aaron clenched his jaw, pursed his lips, squinted his eyes, and stared straight at The Contact's eyes.

"I paid you $10,000 as a non-refundable payment. I want my money's worth. There are some things I'm going to demand, and I'm going to get them. Take…them…off. All…of…them! Now! Throw them over to me!"

"And if I refuse?" The Contact said with a complacent, pompous tone to his voice.

"I will contact the police and tell them I am being blackmailed."

"You cannot tell anyone because I'll tell them all about you," The Contact snapped.

"Excuse me. You just made a pledge to me when I said to you, 'I will comply with your demand, but you have to promise me you will not, and I mean you will never, divulge this to anyone.'" Your response to me was, 'You have my word. I will tell no one, and when I say you have my word, you have my word.' Besides, your fingerprints are probably all over this bag. Do you plan to weasel out? You forget easily Mr. Contact, We shook hands!"

"All right!" The Contact stood, put his pad and pencil on the table next to the sofa, removed his cell phone, his jacket, unbuttoned his shirt, and continued until he was bare-chested. Aaron gave a gesture with the index finger of his left hand just as The Contact did to him indicating to take off his jeans. He removed his boots and socks, undid his belt, and lowered his jeans to his ankles.

"Keep your stupid-looking underwear on and throw the jeans over here," Aaron commanded. "Now give me your cell phone."

The Contact did, and Aaron powered it down. Now he knew he wasn't wired and nothing was being recorded.

"OK, now we're on a level playing field. Get dressed!"

The Contact got dressed, put on his boots, and sat down.

"Now, as I said before I was rudely interrupted, tell me all about this person. I want the whole story, everything. His name, his address and addresses, his habits if you know them, the car he drives, everything. I must present 'The Legionnaire' with an accurate picture. He is my contact in Milan. Like me, you will never know his name, who he is, and you will never meet him. If he accepts the job, I will meet with you to tell you his price, plan, and proposal. If he doesn't accept it, your $10,000 will not be returned. That's my fee."

Aaron wanted this whole fiasco over with. He started to tell the story to The Contact. He described everything he knew in great detail. The Contact sat, hardly looking at Aaron, writing notes on a notepad he had brought. Aaron sat in the chair across from the sofa speaking in a calm and quiet tone; he spoke, thinking about Maria from the beginning of their relationship. The Contact didn't ask any questions. He let

Aaron lead the way and tell his story.

They worked together for more than half an hour. Aaron tried to be as specific and detailed as he could remember. There was a long pause.

"If that's it, I think I have everything I need. Anything else you would like to tell me?" The Contact added.

I can't think of anything right now."

"All right. If you think of something in the next couple of days, put your flag out on your patio as I have seen it there before. I know where you live, and I will check it each day. That will be my sign you want to tell me something. I will contact you by phone, and we will meet at Starbucks again. Nothing is discussed over the phone. Am I clear?"

"Yes, very clear, and I will be aware of your 'people' who accompany you. I will watch just the same as you. Am I clear?"

"Very clear. I will let you know when I give this information to The Legionnaire. He will digest it and reach me in a way you will not know."

The Contact finished dressing, took the gym bag with the money, and departed. No handshake, no "good-bye." He unlatched the chain, opened the door, and left.

Aaron sat still in the chair. Part of him wanted to go back and not go through with this. The other part of him wanted to get rid of Roberto and go on with his life with Maria. But what the hell am I supposed to do? he thought. What am I getting myself into? He dragged his fingers through his hair, sat forward resting his elbows on his knees, his forehead damp with sweat. He got up and started to pace the room. He didn't move to latch the door or put on the security chain. He looked out the window to familiar surroundings. The sun shined in, so he tried to calm down. He went into the bedroom, grabbed the TV remote, and tuned to the NFL game. He settled back on the bed and tried to concentrate on what he had told The Contact.

His thoughts kept coming back to Maria. She is such a lovely woman, he thought, and didn't deserve what was happening to her. What made it so exciting to think about her? She seemed like everything I had been looking for all my life. His abs tightened and he took in a deep breath, tilting his head back remembering being inside of her, the smell of her body, the feel of her embrace, what she felt like the night they made love together in the B&B before she left for Milan. Dammit! He didn't know what to do about her — for her.

Aaron decided he could not stay in the hotel room. He needed to get out, so he dressed and left to get something to eat. He enjoyed a nice quiet dinner at Risottos, an Italian eatery, where he toasted two glasses of a nice Italian red and gave a salute to Maria. It wasn't busy early in the evening so he took his time, finished, and went back to the hotel.

"I can't do this," he said out loud. "I can't stay in this place. I have to go home. I'll come back early in the morning before work and check out." Aaron picked up the gym bag The Contact brought, stuffed the shorts and T-shirt into it, got dressed, and left the hotel. Arriving back at his apartment, he turned on some lights, put a couple of drops of Chanel No. 5 on a handkerchief, set it down next to the computer, and decided to send Maria a note.

She had already written him one.

Oh Aaron, my love. I am having such a terrible time with Roberto. I am— how do you say? — absolutely beside myself? I now know he is seeing someone else. Just today, Sunday, he did not go to me with mass but said he had to go to office. Yeah, right! I know where office is. I went to the IL Ristorante across from the door leading to "friend's" flat. I sat in the window, ordered a cappuccino, and about a half hour later I heard a Vespa coming down the street. It stopped in front of the place. She was riding on the back and Roberto was driving. She wore a pink dress and pink shoes. They parked, he picked her up, laughing and kissing, carrying her into doorway leading to her place and they disappeared, closing the door behind them. This is not his office. I filmed it all on my iPhone. I left and cried all the way home. He called me about 4:30 saying he was tied up with a client and hoped to get away soon. He did not come home until 6:20 p.m. Somehow I have to get rid of him. I cannot live like this any longer. We plan to go to Portofino over Christmas holidays, the 15th through the 1st of January. I will be in touch.

Love U

Aaron replied:

Stay strong. Something will work out for the better. I know it will! I'll write you more later.

Love U 2

Twenty-Five

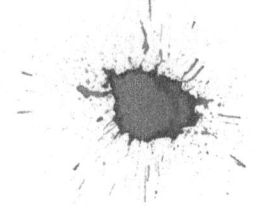

The sun shining brightly made this September day on Sunday morning in Milan warm and pleasant. The chill in the air seemed to disappear. A man sat at a table next to the Galleria Vittorio Emanuele II sipping his cappuccino. He was alone, reading the *E Polis Milano* — the daily newspaper of Milan. He also had a copy of *La Gazzetta dello Sport*, a popular newspaper covering all the sporting events in Italy and elsewhere. The pigeons were active, swirling around and heading toward the Duomo, Milan's magnificent cathedral, the low pitch of the bells ringing at 10:30. The man gazed at the structure with its 4,000 statues on the exterior. He marveled at its construction which began in 1386 and the entire cathedral finally completed with the installation of the main doors in 1944. The 11:00 mass was about to begin with many people entering. The Cardinal Archbishop of Milan always presides at the 11:00 o'clock mass every Sunday, and it is well attended. The Ristorante Terraza Aperol made a perfect spot for viewing the Piazza del Duomo. There were many people strolling about this morning, probably because of the clear sky, warm sun, and the mass at the Duomo. He remained seated, as he did not care to participate in any religious ceremony. He put down his first paper and picked up his copy of *La Gazzetta dello Sport* — a paper he enjoyed more than the local/world news. The server came to his table; he ordered another cappuccino.

His phone rang. It wasn't his cell phone, but a disposable one he carried for different reasons. He would often have private conversations he wished to keep private and untraceable. He reached in his trench-coat pocket and saw it was an overseas call. He answered.

"Buongiorno." (*Good morning.*)

"Buongiorno amico mio." (*Good morning, my friend.*)

"Si chiama molto presto. Non abbiamo parlato per qualche tempo." (*You are calling early. We have not spoken for some time.*)

"Sì lo so." (*Yes, I know.*)

"Questo deve essere una chiamata importante." (*This must be an important call.*)

"Vuoi chiamarti se non fosse stato? Tutte le mie chiamate a voi sono importanti." (*Would I call you if it wasn't? All my calls to you are important.*)

"Lei ha ragione il mio contatto. Appena non ho parlato a voi in qualche tempo." (*You are right, my Contact. I just have not spoken to you in some time.*)

"Sì, e ho un lavoro per voi in Portofino. Possiamo parlare inglese?" (*Yes, and I have a job for you in Portofino. Can we speak English?*)

"Sì certo." (*Yes, of course.*)

They had no problem with understanding English. They both studied at Universities in the United States and spoke the language fluently.

"So how are things with my Legionnaire friend?" The Contact waited for a reply. There was always a delay in the conversation when speaking on a cell phone, and more so overseas with the disposable ones.

"Your Legionnaire friend is just fine, enjoying a nice cappuccino on a bright sunny morning. And, my Contact in the United States, it must be going on 4:00 in the morning. How goes it with you?"

Just then, the bells at the Duomo began to make their loud, booming sound at 10:52, announcing a five-minute warning of the beginning of the mass, making the conversation inaudible. They lasted about three minutes, creating a long pause in communication.

"It never fails. Just when I start an important call, something interrupts," The Legionnaire added.

"Not to worry," replied The Contact. "We always seem to connect just the same. To answer your question, I am doing fine. Yes, it is exactly 4 a.m. here. I am in need of your services. I met a man who has someone in Portofino needing to go on a vacation." "Vacation" was the code word for making them disappear.

"I think it can be arranged," The Legionnaire said. "Portofino is just three hours away. Give me a time frame. I will put it on my calendar. Tell me about it, I'm sure I can handle it. You know my success rate."

"Great!" The Contact said. "I knew you could." He started slowly giving The Legionnaire details as accurately as possible, which Aaron had provided. Sometime between the 1st and the 15th of October. The exchange lasted about 20 minutes with a complete understanding of what was to be done. The fee would be $15,000, or €12,000 euros, half paid up front with the remainder paid within 72 hours after completion, both wired through a special code to The Legionnaire's Swiss bank account.

"Be sure to advise your client what will happen if they do not complete the transaction," The Legionnaire advised.

"I will," said The Contact. "I'll make it very clear. There has not been confusion so far, and I'm sure there'll not be any misunderstanding in the future. This gentleman has much to lose."

The discussion between them ended with The Contact saying, "Tutto è chiaro?" (*All is Clear?*)

"Tutto è chiaro," replied The Legionnaire. "Sì, mi aspetterà per la chiamata. Addio." (*Yes, I will wait for your call. Bye.*)

The conversation ended. The Legionnaire put his phone away and continued to read *La Gazzetta dello Sport*. About 10 minutes later the waiter brought the bill. He put his newspaper away, paid, and started to stroll to his apartment on the Via dei Mercanti.

Approaching his flat, he checked his locked Verde Oliva Fiat Sport 500 parked in front. He had a great affection for the car and especially the color. He would plan to drive to the country later in the afternoon and to Portofino when the time came. He would wait for the final word from The Contact. He entered the building, went up the stairs even though there was an elevator; he liked to stay in shape so he always used the stairs.

Entering his flat, he sensed the warmth of the sun filtering through the windows. He took off his trench coat, walked down the hall toward the bedroom. Just inside the room on the left was his closet. He opened the door. On the back wall there were some moldings covering the corner edges of the wall as well as behind each shelf. The wall looked completely normal. The center shelf had only lightweight clothing stored on it, socks, handkerchiefs, underclothes. He reached, removed the clothing to another area, lifted up on the shelf, and removed it to expose the shelf supports. The right bracket acted as a small lever, when raised, not removed, releasing a sliding door. It looked completely unnoticeable, but no one except The Legionnaire would know of it. It was inconspicuous if anyone were to look in. Behind the moveable panel, unnoticeable to the naked eye, he would keep personal and private possessions. He didn't like some things in open view. "Out of sight, out of mind" was his motto. Everything looked indistinguishable and matching. He lifted the shelf, raised the lever, and it released the plain wall panel, allowing the door to slide open.

He reached in. There was a sizeable amount of cash in U.S. dollars and euros. The one item he wanted right now was his Beretta 92 FS 9mm pistol. He hadn't used it for some time, but knew what someone meant when they used the word "vacation." The Italians never used the word "vacation" as in the United States; it was "holiday" in Italy. He liked to go to the firing range for practice and keep his proficiency but hadn't been there for some time. He had friends who would go, meeting them and enjoying an hour or so of pistol practice. He liked this weapon for several reasons. First of all, it's made in Italy. It's double/single action, external manual safety, docking lever. It was lightweight, made from aircraft-quality aluminum alloy. He also had a silencer when necessary. He decided to go to the range and practice his skills.

He closed the panel, replaced the shelf on the brackets, and put the clothing back where it was before. He changed into clothing more suitable, took a box of shells, his Beretta, packed them in a briefcase, and went down to his car. He locked the briefcase in the trunk, got in, and headed to the firing range.

Twenty-Six

Aaron suddenly awakened. Nothing caused it. He just opened his eyes. He looked at the clock. It was 5:43 a.m. The alarm would go off at 6:00 so he turned it off and sat up on the edge of the bed. He went to his computer. There was a message from Maria.

What can I say except, I wish I was with you. Or, maybe it would be nice if it was you here with me. I do miss you very much. I cannot get you off my mind. I learned quite a lot from you. Our time together was so short, and I am ready to leave Roberto. He has been so distant from me and gives me no courtesy. We are planning on going to the villa in Portofino in a couple of weeks from the 1st through the 15th of October. I think I told you that before.

Aaron's phone rang, interrupting the e-mail. It was 5:56. Again, the caller ID read, "*Private Number Unknown Name.*" His thoughts immediately turned to The Contact. He picked it up.

"Hello, this is Aaron." A delay occurred, but he did not hang up.

"Good morning. I am calling about further assistance in your Milan inquiry."

"Yes, what information do you have for me?" Aaron responded.

"Meet me tonight at 7:00; Starbucks. Have $7,500 in your checking account and bring a blank check with you. I will be alone." He hung up. Aaron didn't have a chance to tell him they would be there the 1st through the 15th so he put out his flag.

He sat frozen not only by Maria's message, which he had not

finished, but also by the abruptness of the call from The Contact. It bothered him in both directions — Maria and The Contact.

He went back to the e-mail.

Now he tells me he has to go into Milan on Fridays and possibly on Tuesdays as well. He says, "meetings." I know what kind of meetings he is planning. I want to leave, I want to get out of here. I wish he were gone for good. Today I plan on going to the palestra. Oh, it means the gym where you are.

I love you, and I miss you. I know we will meet again.
Maria

Aaron decided to clean up, have some coffee and a bagel, and get to the bus stop. He shaved, thinking how his life has changed. It appeared he was in this for the long haul. He would try to have a good day at the clinic, maybe stop at Jake's for a quick one and then head to Starbucks. The cool air was refreshing during his walk to the bus. No "Good Morning." New driver.

He arrived at the clinic at 7:30 and reviewed his appointments for the day. It would be busy. If this is going to work, let's get it finished. What if I'm caught? What if there's a witness? What if this just simply doesn't work? I have to get this off my mind and concentrate on the job at hand: my patients.

The day wore on and seemed to drag. Aaron hoped it would be a businesslike meeting at Starbucks and not confrontational like it was at the hotel. He went out for lunch, alone, to a quiet restaurant he enjoyed when he needed some peace. He had the special, fish and chips, followed by a cup of coffee, and left to go back to the clinic.

4:30 came, and the clinic closed. On his way out the receptionist stopped him and said, "Dr. Kelley, is everything all right?"

"Yes, Bridget. Why do you ask?"

"You have not seemed yourself. You're quiet, a little withdrawn. I'm sorry. It's none of my business, but I have seen a change in you. And, by the way, your sister Sharon called and wanted you to give her a call concerning Thanksgiving."

"Thanksgiving? A month and a half away, my sister, always on top of things and planning ahead. Thanks, Bridget, for caring. I am all right, just in deep thought about one of my investments. If it doesn't work out, I have a lot to lose. I will give Sharon a call. Good night."

"G'night, Dr. Kelley." Aaron turned around and smiled at Bridget.

"Also, Bridget, we have known each other for several years. When we're meeting without patients present, please address me as Aaron," he said with a smile on his face and a gentle raising of his left hand.

Bridget nodded, smiled and said, "Thank you, Aaron."

Twenty-Seven

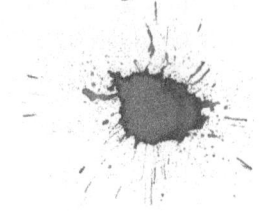

Jake's was busy, but not crowded. His usual table was free, so he sat down and took out his iPhone. A few seconds later Max brought the scotch, rocks, twist.

"Hey, Aaron, haven't seen you as regular as you used to be. Been busy?"

"Yeah, Max, lots goin' on, but I'll be back on my routine soon."

"Good," Max replied. "It's always good to see you."

Max turned, headed back behind the bar while Aaron turned on his phone: no messages. The scotch tasted good after a busy day. His thoughts turned to Maria, Roberto, and The Contact. What does he want? When he calls, he abruptly hangs up. It gave me no clue. He finished and went to Luigi's, got a piece of pizza and a small salad. Finishing, it was now 6:48, so he decided he had better get going.

He walked into Starbucks and took the table they had occupied on their original meeting. At 6:59, The Contact walked in and came to the table. He was alone. No one trailed in after him. No greeting, no handshake, just a business approach of what would happen. He sat down and started.

Aaron abruptly started, I put my flag out, but you did not call."

"I saw it but knew we were meeting tonight. What is your message?"

"They will be in Portofino between the 1st and the 15th of October."

"I will let The Legionnaire know."

"I notified The Legionnaire, and he will take on the job; $15,000 payable one-half now and the balance upon completion. It will happen sometime between the 1st and the 15th as you have told me, I can assure

84 •

you. You will not know when, what, or how. He will let me know when Roberto has gone on 'vacation.' Did you bring a blank check with your account number on it?"

"Yes, I did," replied Aaron.

The Contact opened his laptop computer and logged on. He went to the Internet page and brought up **The National Bank of Switzerland**.com. He entered a user ID, then the password. The screen asked for which bank and its location. Having selected it, he entered the user ID for the Swiss bank, the account number, and the eight-digit code for the transfer. He turned the computer to face Aaron. The screen asked for "from" and Aaron typed in his bank ID number. The website searched and confirmed his bank. He entered his password then account number. *Amount?* Aaron typed 7,500.00. *Currency?* United States Dollars. He pressed "enter." A message appeared: *Once you start this transaction, it cannot be stopped. Are you sure you wish to continue?* Aaron pressed "enter." The screen went blank and after about 10 seconds, "processing transaction" appeared. 20 seconds later a message appeared: "transaction complete."

The Contact was very gruff and matter-of-fact. "We will receive a confirmation when The Legionnaire has completed his work and we will do this exact same process. *Capire?*"

"Yes, I understand and have a question," Aaron said.

"No questions," said The Contact as he gruffly got up, closed his computer, walked to the side door, and left.

Aaron left Starbucks and walked to his apartment building. His thoughts turned to his future. *I can never divulge to Maria anything — nothing; nada; nicht! I love her so much and am eager to see her. Roberto is such an ass. As soon as this is over, I'm going to see to it she comes here. In the meantime, I must write her so she wakes up to some good news.*

Twenty-Eight

Saturday, October 1

The Legionnaire called The Belmond Hotel Splendido across from the Villa Lugari Cinque Terra in Portofino and made a reservation, arriving Sunday, October 2nd through the 15th. He'd stayed there before. A front room with a separate bedroom would be ideal, confirmed at €140/night. The hotel had a terrace, swimming pool, pastel-colored rooms, a gym, sauna, tennis courts, and extensive gardens. The view would give him access to the street Roberto apparently walked down every morning to get his paper and cigar. The Legionnaire knew what Roberto looked like, as Aaron had given The Contact the picture he had taken at Jake's one evening and he had passed it on to him.

On Sunday, he packed his bag, read the morning paper, and had some lunch including his usual espresso. The drive would be about three hours. He would be sure to stay at or under the speed limit of 112 km/hour knowing he had his Beretta 92 FS 9mm pistol with him. He did not need the Polizia stopping him. The day, sunny and warm, made Portofino a nice change of scenery. Check-in was not before 3:00 p.m., so he decided to take his time, leave around noon, and stop along the way.

The car ran beautifully. He loved it, and besides, it was very popular in Italy, so he would be unnoticed. The A7 from Milan to Genova was its usual heavy truck traffic. The Legionnaire set his cruise control to 110 km/hour so he was just under the speed limit. He took the

Tortona exit, went into the roadside café at the edge of town to relax for a bit and have a cappuccino. There was warmth in the air and the pleasantness of the countryside. Tortona is about halfway to Portofino so his Garmin indicated he would arrive about 3:30.

Going through Genova is not easy with no bypass of the city, and the truck traffic made everything come to a crawl. He did not worry and was quite patient as he had no schedule to meet. Passing Genova, the road paralleled the Mediterranean. With the sun shining and the air warm, he lowered his window to enjoy it. He took the E80, the road from Genova to Rome. It was four lanes with many tunnels. The traffic was light leaving Genova, so he made good time. He took the exit at Recco and went to the road paralleling the sea. It was a scenic, beautiful, and relaxing route.

He arrived in Portofino at 3:35 p.m. in 74° weather and went straight to the hotel. He had let his beard grow somewhat but neatly trimmed. Before he got out of the car, he put on wire-rimmed glasses with thick clear glass, a custom-made toupee over his thin, balding hair. He exited the car, put on a special-made vest, which made him look a little paunchy and overweight. He pulled his sleeve on the left arm to display a fake tattoo he'd put on before leaving Milan. It was water resistant and only be removed with a special soap he brought along, and would do so when he finished the job before he left the hotel. He finished off with a black generic baseball cap with no logo — a disguise without defects. After he completed his work, he would dispose of the cap at a road stop on his way back to Milan, followed at another stop to destroy the glasses with a hammer he kept in a tool kit in the trunk and dispose of them. The other items he would keep in his flat for possible future use.

He went to the front desk. They were expecting him, and his accommodation request for a room on the second floor facing the street was no problem. This time of year was quieter than the summer months. He opened the door to room 206 and found it quite satisfactory: living room and separate bedroom. The Villa Lugari Cinque Terra was directly across the street and he had an excellent view.

He unpacked, showered, changed clothes, put on his disguise, and went out for a walk to become acquainted with the surroundings, the news shop, and the Tabaccheria — the tobacco store. The day proved to be productive. He found the two places he wanted and went in both. The time of day, and being Sunday, it was busy. People did notice him as he wore the thick glasses and heard one child tell his mother, "Guarda, mamma. Che l'uomo ha grandi occhi." (*Look, Mama. The man has big eyes.*)

"Guido, che non è educato." (*Guido, that is not polite.*)

"Mi scuso," she said. (*I apologize.*)

The Legionnaire nodded his head and smiled at the child.

Back at the hotel, he unpacked his Beretta 92 FS pistol and silencer. He liked the design as it made for easy cleaning. The hard-chromed barrel ensured smooth feeding and ejection of ammunition. It was lightweight and easily concealed in his clothing. He never had any personal complaints about it and enjoyed his time at the shooting gallery to stay proficient, and proficient and accurate he was.

He took a short nap and headed out for dinner.

Twenty-Nine

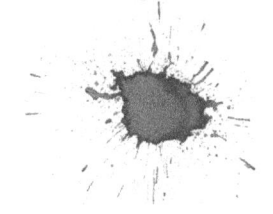

Monday, October 3

Morning came. The Legionnaire woke early. He put the coffee on which the hotel had provided in the room. The morning paper was outside his door; he picked it up, and when the coffee finished brewing, he sat down and started to read, keeping an eye on The Villa. About 6:25 a.m., a man appeared across the street. It wasn't very light out but was enough to make out his features. He came from the Villa Lugari Cinque Terra. He was tall, lean, dark haired. Could it be him? Roberto? He put his paper down, dressed in his disguise and jogging attire. He left the hotel.

The sun, rising in a clear blue sky, made the Mediterranean sparkle to the west. It was cool this morning but not cold. He walked to the news shop three blocks away. The cobblestone street made the footing unsteady, but he enjoyed the old-world atmosphere. He entered the shop, and sure enough it was Roberto. He very carefully and nonchalantly bumped into him. They turned to each other, and each said, "Mi Scusi." (*Excuse me*). The Legionnaire had a close-up view of the face. It was indeed Roberto, unshaven but with the same features as in the photo taken at Jake's which The Contact provided.

The Legionnaire left the shop, having bought a couple of papers and a magazine. He headed down the street to the Tabaccheria. He assumed as briefed, Roberto would come in and buy his cigar. Moments later, Roberto entered the shop.

"Buongiorno, Roberto. È bello rivederti. Come stai?" (*Good morning,*

Roberto. It's good to see you again. How are you?)

"Grazie. È bello vederti. Sto bene." (*Thank you. It's good to see you. I am fine.*)

"Quanto tempo si sarà qui?" (*How long will you be here?*)

"Circa dieci giorni. Devo tornare a Milano domani, ma tornerà il mercoledì." (*About 10 days. I have to go back to Milan tomorrow, but I will return on Wednesday.*)

"Vuoi che il tuo solito cubano?" (*Do you want your usual Cuban?*)

"Sì in effetti." (*Yes, indeed.*)

The Legionnaire took it all in as Roberto selected his Cuban cigar from a fresh shipment the owner said had just arrived. He now had Roberto's early footsteps and pattern observed, and it was exactly what The Contact provided him. He left the shop with Roberto and the owner in conversation and headed back to the hotel. He sat in the window of his room, no lights on, and waited to see where Roberto went when he came to The Villa. About ten minutes later, Roberto appeared with his unlit Cuban in his mouth. He didn't go in the front door of The Villa but down a walk and steps to the left side. He disappeared in a door halfway down.

The Legionnaire left and walked to the Trattoria Dei Pescatori for some breakfast. This should be easy, he thought, but he had to put a plan together.

Thirty

Tuesday, October 4

Morning came, and again, The Legionnaire got up early, decided to dress right away into disguise, make the coffee, pick up the paper outside his door, but this time he put the paper down on the table next to his chair. He grabbed a cup of coffee, put on his hairpiece, cap, and glasses, walked to the lobby and out onto the street.

"Buongiorno," the desk clerk said as he passed by.

"Buongiorno," The Legionnaire responded with a wave of his hand, smiled, and walked out the door.

About 6:30, a late-model BMW came out of the car park beneath the building of The Villa. It was difficult to recognize the driver as the sun was not up even though it was light out, the windows of the car were tinted. The Legionnaire watched as the car stopped in front of the news shop. He walked slowly and figured it was Roberto because he knew he was going to Milan. There were several people on the street — joggers, dog walkers, and couples at this hour — so he wasn't conspicuous. The man he was keeping an eye on left the news shop and went into the Tabaccheria and didn't stay long, but long enough for The Legionnaire to move closer to the car to get a view. The man left the shop. It was Roberto. He didn't have a cigar in his mouth, but it was in his right hand. He climbed into the car and drove off. Now it would be time to explore and set the plan he had worked out in his mind at dinner last night.

As he walked back toward his hotel, he observed a taxi

slowly approaching The Villa where Roberto and Maria were staying. He walked unhurriedly to appear plain, uninterested, and ordinary. He strolled for a moment, waiting to see who the taxi was picking up. He was about a car length away. The driver got out of the car and went up to the stairs where Roberto entered and exited; a woman approached. He heard her say to the driver, "La stazione ferroviaria" (*the train station*), and got into the taxi. She never looked his way so she never saw him. He wondered if it was Maria. The taxi sped away so he stopped at a local trattoria for some coffee and a breakfast roll.

Back at the hotel, he decided to go to a Negozio di Liquori to buy a very nice bottle of wine. He went to The Villa first. Approaching the desk clerk, he said he wanted to contact either Maria or Roberto Beldenado but he did not know their room number. The clerk said they were in suite 104A. The Legionnaire went to the house phone and called but did not receive an answer. The desk clerk gestured to him and told him they had both gone to Milan. Maria would return tonight and Roberto in the morning. He left The Villa and went back to his hotel, picked up a bottle of wine, and put it in a nice package. He walked across the street and went down the side steps next to The Villa. It was a security door, so he waited. A few minutes later, someone opened the door to exit. He faked it and fidgeted with his hand in his pocket, saying, "Grazie, mi stavo appena fuori la mia chiave." (*Thank you, I was just getting out my key.*)

"Buongiorno. Sono felice di aiutarvi. Mi consenta." (*Good morning; glad to help you. Allow me.*)

The gentleman held the door open for him and he walked down the hall to room 104A. He knocked on the door, and if someone answered, he would acknowledge he had the wrong room. No one answered. He walked around the corner. A maid was cleaning the room.

"Mi Scusi. Ho lasciato la mia chiave nella mia stanza. Puoi aiutarmi?" (*Excuse me. I left my key in my room. Can you help me?*)

"Che stanza sei?" (*What room are you in?*)

"Uno zero quattro A," he replied. (*One zero four A.*)

"Come si chiama?" (*What is your name?*)

"Roberto, Roberto Beldenado."

The maid checked the listing of occupants and found his name; she unlocked the door and allowed him to enter. "Grazie," he said. He went in the room and closed the door.

The Legionnaire wanted to see the layout and access to the patio from the outside. It was indeed a beautiful suite, and the connection via a path from the front would be easy access. He left the bottle of wine on the kitchen counter with a note reading:

Sono contento che sei qui. Questo ospite mistero sarà essere contatto con voi in un paio di giorni con una sorpresa. (I'm glad you are here. This mystery guest will be contacting you in a couple of days with a surprise.)

Having completed his inspection, he knew what his plan would be.

Thirty-One

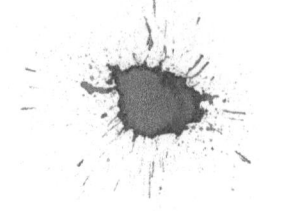

Aaron awakened early and did his usual routine. He went to his computer but there was only one message from Maria written at 6:45 a.m. — 12:45 a.m. where Aaron lived.

> *My love — I am going to Milan today to do some shopping, but mainly to check up on Roberto. He left a few minutes ago, driving. I leave via taxi for the train station. The Milan express departs at 7:45. I will return this evening and write you when I get back. I love you and want to see you, be with you and touch you. I want this to happen soon. I feel so sad.*
>
> con tanto amore,

He didn't write back as he knew she'd left for the day, so he would write her this evening when he returned from work and the gym. So much was going through Aaron's head. He just didn't know why he'd gotten himself into this, but he was halfway, and he knew he couldn't turn back. The coffee tasted good. He took the cup with him on his way to the bus. The usual bus driver was back, giving his usual "Good morning, Aaron." Aaron smiled and took his seat, sipping his coffee and enjoying the beautiful October morning with fall colors on the trees.

His day went well with the usual patients coming in after a summer in the sun. He did a biopsy on one he felt sure was a melanoma. He spent his lunch hour with a colleague from the office. After closing at 4:30, he went to the gym and did his usual workout. Afterword, he went to Jake's on the way home. This was not typical for him. He couldn't get Maria off his mind. He missed her and her wonderful Chanel No. 5. Max presented him with his Chivas, rocks, twist. Aaron thanked him, took a sip, and stared at the table where Maria always sat. After he finished, he walked home. He sat down at his computer.

7:15 p.m. – 2:15 a.m. Milan. Maria — I miss you so much and have felt terrible about what is happening to you and to me. I hope we can meet soon and be together; just together, you and me. I have done some strange things lately, not like me at all. There is no way I can convey to you my thoughts and ambitions. I would just like us to be together forever. Someday when we are hand-in-hand, I can tell you my feelings and what I have done recently in my life. But I did it all for you. It is so unlike me but I will have to live with it until death do I part. All I can say for now is, please forgive me. Roberto can go his way and be with whomever he chooses. You can also go your way and be with me. To bed now; someday, we shall meet again.

Looking forward,
Aaron

Thirty-Two

Wednesday October 5

Morning came on a bright sunny October day. Aaron got up and poured himself a cup of coffee. He picked up the paper at the front door of his condominium and went to his computer. A note from Maria was in his mailbox.

> *Aaron, I received your e-mail, and I am completely puzzled. I can't think for the life of me what you are meaning. I went to Milan today and am heading for bed. It's late and Roberto won't be here until about 11 a.m. tomorrow, that is if he comes. I browsed through The Galleria and walked to the Caffetteria across from where I saw Roberto before. His car was parked in front, but I did not see him. I waited for some time, but he never showed. He was probably very busy, if you know what I mean.*

The phone rang. A chill went up Aaron's spine. At 6 a.m., who would call me except... He looked at the caller I.D. and it read, "*Private Number Unknown Name.*" He hated to answer but knew he had to.

"Hello."

"I saw your lights on, so I knew you were up. Meet me at Starbucks tonight at 7 p.m. The balance on your Milan trip is due. Make sure you have the amount deposited in your checking account. The procedure will be the same as last time." He hung up.

It was a difficult time for Aaron. A chill went up his spine and he somehow wished this had never happened. Can anything be traced? I shall have to live with this forever, he thought. He knew Roberto was dead, or as The Legionnaire said it, "He went on vacation." If it all went smoothly, I will be with Maria in a short time. He went back to his e-mail from her.

> *I had to leave to catch the 4:30 train, the TrenItalia High Speed Express to Genova and then Portofino. I want to arrive before Roberto. It's fast and takes about two hours. I had dinner on the train. Started with a good martini to relax me. I never drink them but I thought it time. I am now here and am going to bed. Do not let anything get you down. Soon we will be together.*
>
> *Ti amo,*
> *Maria*

Thirty-Three

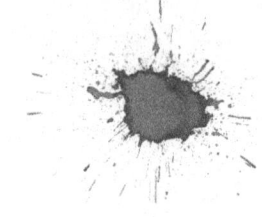

Aaron spent his day as usual and tried to get the excitement as well as the "vacation of Roberto" off his mind. He had his usual lunch, but alone today, just him and his cellphone. He went online to his bank and transferred the $7,500 into his checking account. The clinic closed at 4:30 and all he could think of was the finale. He thought he would just forget about all of it. Roberto got what he deserved. Maria would be his, and they would all live happily ever after.

Jake's was its customary buzz at 5 p.m. He received his usual drink and he saluted The Legionnaire. He would never meet him, know his name, or even know what he looked like. The only person he knew was The Contact and what he looked like. No name, no phone number. The only thing he remembered was he wore stupid-looking underwear. This was all behind him now and he was keeping it locked away in the cobwebs of his mind. He ordered another Chivas, rocks, twist — his usual libation. It was now after 6 o'clock, and he went to the deli across the street, had a sandwich and a cup of coffee. He left at 6:45 and went to Starbucks. The Contact was not there but at 6:59 he walked in the front door. Approaching the same table as twice before, he did not greet Aaron and did not stop for a coffee, but proceeded to open his computer. The same information was entered as before: name of bank, password, bank in Switzerland (a different one this time), the password provided and entered by The Contact (also different); Aaron entered the $7,500, pressed "enter." The screen went blank and about 30 seconds later a message came up: "transaction complete."

The Contact started to close his computer.

"So how did it go?" Aaron asked.

"As planned by The Legionnaire," he replied.

"Can't you tell me anything about it?"

The Contact got up, computer in hand, pressed his bottom against the door to open it.

"I know nothing about how he did his work. The only thing I know is a woman came on the scene when he did the job."

Aaron sat up, got a long face, put up his hands palms up, level with his shoulders, and said, "Wha— What, wait a minute, you… tell me, I don't understand, I want to know what happened." Aaron was clearly agitated.

"There is nothing for you to understand. All The Legionnaire said was she was wearing a yellow dress. However, do not worry, my friend; nothing will be traced. He sent them both 'on vacation.' You got two for the price of one." The Contact pushed the door open and disappeared.

Epilogue

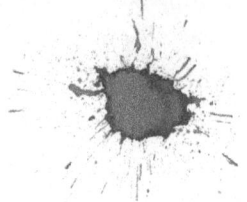

Thank you for buying my first work of fiction. I hope you enjoyed it as much as I enjoyed writing it.

Til Death Do us Part is entirely a work of fiction. Many Names of places, cities, streets, restaurants, etc. are real, but only used with the intention of creating a fictional story line. It takes place in the United States, St. John in the Virgin Islands and Italy. You may have noticed the city in the U.S. is not mentioned. It could be Pittsburgh, Philadelphia, Boston, or Richmond. You be the judge. There is a buried clue which gives it away and if you discover it, let me know.

If you enjoyed my first work, feel free to drop me a note – good, bad, or indifferent.

If you did not enjoy my first work, feel free to drop me a note – good, bad or indifferent.

I would love to hear from you. It's all part of the educational process.

Rois4richo@gmail.com (R O is for Rich O)

In the subject line please write, "Til Death Do Us Part."

I am currently working on my next book. It has a double twist surprise.